AND SURROUNDING
~TERRITORIES~
D1649096
NAOGIZAGA
THE BANNER OF
GHATAN
Helkothan
Kokozritzaga
GHATAN
CRAGMANTLE
TORGAR
Zutteznа
SKAROR
Akamazim Forest
Tegaarn Mtns
Blackshroud Trail
WAR BANNER OF
THE
HAMMERLANDS
0
50
100
150
SCALE IN MILES
WASTELAND
VOLCANOES
SWAMP

The bearer of this scroll, namely,
is an initiate in the disciplines of the Kai

Trumpets announce the advance and you set off across the body-strewn battlefield with a force 900 strong. Pikemen lead the column with archers close behind, and bringing up the rear are a levy of militia, many of whom lived in Cetza before Drakkarim invaded. Their moral is high for this is their chance to recover their homes and their land.

Tensely you watch as the enemy attack. The Palace Guard link shields but, as the Hammerlanders slam into their line, they buckle and waver beneath the crushing onslaught. As your force crosses the ditch, you pray that the Prince and his men have strength enough to hold for just a few minutes more . . .

JOE DEVER was born in 1956 at Woodford Bridge in Essex, England. After he left college, he became a professional musician, working in studios in Europe and America. While working in Los Angeles in 1977, he discovered a game called "Dungeons and Dragons" and was soon an enthusiastic player. Five years later he won the Advanced Dungeons and Dragons Championship in the US, where he was the only British competitor. The Lone Wolf adventures are the culmination of many years of developing the world of Magnamund. They are printed in several languages and sold all over the world.

Joe Dever Books From Berkley Publishing

The Lone Wolf Series:
Flight from the Dark
Fire on the Water
The Caverns of Kalte
The Chasm of Doom
Shadow on the Sand
The Kingdoms of Terror
Castle Death
The Jungle of Horrors
The Cauldron of Fear
The Dungeons of Torgar
The Prisoners of Time
The Masters of Darkness
The Plague Lords of Ruel
The Captives of Kaag
The Darke Crusade
The Legacy of Vashna

The World of Lone Wolf Series:
Grey Star the Wizard
The Forbidden City
Beyond the Nightmare Gate
War of the Wizards

The Freeway Warrior Series:
High Holocaust
Mountain Run
The Omega Zone
California Countdown

by Joe Dever and John Grant

The Legends of Lone Wolf Series:
Eclipse of the Kai
The Dark Door Opens
The Tides of Treachery
The Sword of the Sun
Hunting Wolf

by Joe Dever and Gary Chalk

The Magnamund Companion:
The Complete Guide to the
World of Lone Wolf and
Grey Star

BOOK 10

The Dungeons of Torgar

Joe Dever

Illustrated by Brian Williams

BERKLEY BOOKS, NEW YORK

This Berkley book contains the complete text of the original edition.

THE DUNGEONS OF TORGAR

A Berkley Book, published by arrangement with Century Hutchinson Ltd.

PRINTING HISTORY
Beaver Books edition published 1987
Berkley edition / July 1988

For information address: Arrow Books Limited, 62-65 Chandos Place, London WC2N 4NW.

ISBN: 0-425-10930-5
RL: 9.5

BERKLEY®
Berkley Books are published by
The Berkley Publishing Group,
200 Madison Avenue, New York, New York 10016.
BERKLEY and the "B" design
are trademarks belonging to Berkley Publishing Corporation.

PRINTED IN THE UNITED STATES OF AMERICA

15 14 13 12 11 10 9 8 7

To Glen and Mads

MAGNAKAI DISCIPLINES NOTES

1	Weaponmastery
2	Huntmastery
3	Psi-Surge
4	Curing 4th Magnakai discipline if you have completed 1 Magnakai adventure successfully
5	Divination 5th Magnakai discipline if you have completed 2 Magnakai adventures successfully
6	Psi-Shield 6th Magnakai discipline if you have completed 3 Magnakai adventures successfully
7	Nexus 7th Magnakai discipline if you have completed 4 Magnakai adventures successfully

MAGNAKAI LORE - CIRCLE BONUSES

	CS	EP		CS	EP
CIRCLE OF FIRE	+1	+2	CIRCLE OF SOLARIS	+1	+3
CIRCLE OF LIGHT	0	+3	CIRCLE OF THE SPIRIT	+3	+3

BACKPACK (max. 8 articles)	MEALS
1 Healing Potion (+4EP)	
2 Rope	
3 Blanket	— 3 EP if no Meal available when instructed to eat.
4 Vial of Blue Pills	BELT POUCH Containing Gold Crowns (50 maximum)
5 Flask of Water	
6 Healing Potion (+4EP)	50
7	
8 Can be discarded when not in combat.	

CS = COMBAT SKILL EP = ENDURANCE POINTS

ACTION CHART

COMBAT SKILL

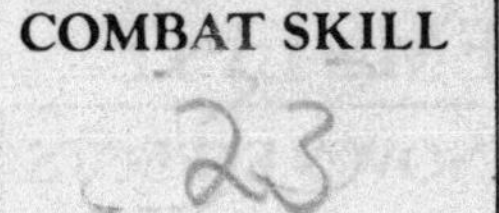

ENDURANCE POINTS

38

Can never go above initial score
0 = dead

COMBAT RECORD

ENDURANCE POINTS LONE WOLF	COMBAT RATIO	ENDURANCE POINTS ENEMY
38	+5	36

MAGNAKAI RANK

SPECIAL ITEMS LIST

DESCRIPTION	KNOWN EFFECTS
Chainmail	+4 EP
Shield	+2 cs
3 Quivers	
Firesphere	
Graveweed Potion	Causes death
11 Fireseeds	
Giak Scroll	
Gray Crystal Ring	
Psi Ring	
Signet Ring	
Medal	

WEAPONS LIST

WEAPONS (maximum 2 Weapons)
1 Sommerswerd
2 Silver Oak Bow: +3
If holding Weapon and appropriate Weaponmastery in combat +3 CS. If combat entered carrying no Weapon −4CS.

WEAPONMASTERY CHECKLIST

DAGGER	√	SPEAR	
MACE		SHORT SWORD	√
WARHAMMER		BOW	√
AXE	√	SWORD	√
QUARTERSTAFF	√	BROADSWORD	√

QUIVER & ARROWS

Quiver	No. of arrows carried
(YES)/NO	18

THE STORY SO FAR

You are the warrior, Lone Wolf, last of the Kai masters of Sommerlund and sole survivor of the massacre that destroyed your kinsmen during a bitter war with your age-old enemies – the Darklords of Helgedad.

Many centuries have passed since Sun Eagle, the first of your kind, established the Order of the Kai. Aided by the magicians of Dessi, he completed a perilous quest to find seven crystals of power known as the Lorestones of Nyxator, and upon their discovery he unlocked a wisdom and strength that lay within both the Lorestones and himself. He recorded the nature of his discoveries and his experiences in a great tome entitled *The Book of the Magnakai*. You have discovered this lost Kai treasure and have given a solemn pledge to restore the Kai to their former glory, thereby ensuring the security of your land in the years to come. However, your diligent study of this ancient book has enabled you to master only three of the ten Magnakai Disciplines. To fulfil your pledge, you must complete the quest first undertaken by Sun Eagle over a thousand years ago. By doing so successfully, you, too, will acquire the power and wisdom of the Magnakai, which is held within the Lorestones' crystal forms.

Already your quest has taken you far from your northern homeland. Following in the footsteps of the first Kai Grand Master, you journeyed to Dessi and sought the help of the Elder Magi, the magicians who aided Sun Eagle on his quest long ago. There you learned that for centuries the Elder Magi had awaited your coming. An ancient Dessi legend tells of the birth and rise to greatness of two 'koura-tas-kai', which means 'sons of the sun'. One was named Ikar, which means 'eagle', and the other was named Skarn, which means 'wolf'. A prophecy foretold that the koura-tas-kai would each come from the north to seek the counsel of the Elder Magi in order that they might fulfil a great quest. Although separated by several centuries, they would share one spirit, one purpose and one destiny – to triumph over the champions of darkness in an age of great peril. The Elder Magi knew that you were Skarn – the wolf of Dessi legend – and in keeping with their ancient vows they promised to help you complete the Magnakai quest.

In Elzian, the capital of Dessi, you were tutored in the histories of Magnamund and received lessons in lore that you would have learned from the Kai masters if only they, like you, had survived the murderous Darklord attack on the Kai monastery twelve years ago. You were eager to learn all that your tutor, Lord Rimoah, could teach you in preparation for the next stage of your quest, but grim news from the Darklands cut short your tuition. In the Darklord city of Helgedad a civil war had erupted, following your defeat of Haakon, Archlord of the Black City. After five years, the battle for the throne of Helgedad had finally been won by a Darklord called Gnaag. The other Darklords, now united behind this new leader, were ordered to amass huge armies in preparation for the conquest of Magnamund. Swiftly their Giak legions grew in number, enabling Gnaag to launch a sweeping invasion that was to catch the freelands unprepared. Several countries, after brief but futile resistance, were completely overrun by Darklord armies; others surrendered without fighting in the face of their determined might. And sadly there were others who chose to betray former friends and allies by joining the Darklord cause, in the misguided hope that they would share in the spoils of victory, following the triumph of Darklord Gnaag. One such land was Vassagonia, a powerful desert realm to the north of Dessi. Her armies mobilized and invaded the neighbouring states of Casiorn and Cloeasia, then marched west through the republic of Anari in order to join with Gnaag's horde as it steamrollered across central Magnamund. The Elder Magi urged you to begin the quest for the fourth Lorestone at once. The enemy armies were converging on the Anarian capital of Tahou, and beneath that ancient city the Lorestone lay hidden.

Aided by Magemaster Banedon, an old friend and fellow countryman, you set off in haste for Tahou and arrived barely hours ahead of the enemy. Successfully you made your descent and discovered the object of your quest, but on returning to the surface you found Tahou transformed into a blazing inferno. Darklord Gnaag and Zakhan Kimah, the ruler of Vassagonia, had learnt of your presence and were determined to destroy you at all costs. For days their engines of war had hurled fire and rock across the walls of Tahou with devastating effect. Then a massive assault, led by the Zakhan himself, breached the west gate and gained entry to the burning city. Armed with a weapon of awesome power, the evil Zakhan sought you out and challenged you to a fight to the death. The struggle was desperate but you emerged victorious and led the Anarians in a counter-attack that cleared the city of the invading foe. The allies of Anari arrived to raise the siege and in the ensuing battle the demoralized armies of Gnaag and Kimah were smashed and routed.

Your defeat of Zakhan Kimah turned the tide of war decisively against the Darklord armies and paved the way for the liberation of the lands they had taken by force. But the sweet taste of victory turned sour when you discovered that Darklord Gnaag had captured the last three remaining Lorestones of Nyxator. Lord Rimoah and other members of the High Council of the Elder Magi joined you in Tahou to help formulate a plan of action. They had already received word from Prince Graygor, the ruler of Eru, that one of his patrols had found a man near the borders of the Hellswamp. He was a Talestrian soldier who had escaped from the dread city-fortress of Torgar where he had been imprisoned after being captured in battle. He had suffered terribly at the hands of the Drakkarim – evil humans in the service of the Darklords – and when found he was so badly injured that he was almost unrecognizable. Before he died he spoke of three radiant gems filled with golden light that had been brought to Torgar from the Darklord city of Mozgôar.

'We are now sure that what he saw was the arrival of the stolen Lorestones,' said Rimoah, speaking on behalf of the High Council. 'They radiate a goodness so strong that Gnaag could not hold them in the Darklands but had to move them to Torgar. There his sorcerers – the Nadziranim – are searching for the means to destroy them. The black art of the Nadziranim has grown powerful of late and we fear they may achieve the task set them by Gnaag. Therefore we must act quickly and with utmost secrecy if the Lorestones and the Magnakai quest are to be saved.'

The Elder Magi had already made preparations for your secret journey to Eru where, upon your arrival, Prince Graygor will help you reach the grim city of Torgar. The thought of having to enter the terrible Drakkarim stronghold fills you with dread, but your pledge to destroy the Darklords and restore the Kai strengthens your resolve and helps you suppress your fear.

On the eve of your journey to Eru, the Elder Magi convene a special meeting of the High Council to pray for the success of your mission. For several hours they kneel in prayer until finally they arise and intone the blessing that has sustained you in the past: 'May the gods Ishir and Kai protect you on your journey into darkness, Kor-Skarn.'

THE GAME RULES

You keep a record of your adventure on the *Action Chart* that you will find in the front of this book. For further adventuring you can copy out the chart yourself or get it photocopied.

During your training as a Kai Master you have developed fighting prowess – COMBAT SKILL – and physical stamina – ENDURANCE. Before you set off on your adventure you need to measure how effective your training has been. To do this take a pencil and, with your eyes closed, point with the blunt end of it on to the *Random Number Table* on the last page of this book. If you pick *0* it counts as zero.

The first number that you pick from the *Random Number Table* in this way represents your COMBAT SKILL. Add 10 to the number you picked and write the total in the COMBAT SKILL section of your *Action Chart* (ie, if your pencil fell on the number 4 in the *Random Number Table* you would enter a COMBAT SKILL of 14). When you fight, your COMBAT SKILL will be pitted against that of your enemy. A high score in this section is therefore very desirable.

The second number that you pick from the *Random Number Table* represents your powers of ENDURANCE. Add 20 to this number and write the total in the ENDURANCE section of your *Action Chart* (ie, if your pencil fell on the number 6 on the *Random Number Table* you would have 26 ENDURANCE points).

If you are wounded in combat you will lose ENDURANCE points. If at any time your ENDURANCE points fall to zero, you are dead and the adventure is over. Lost ENDURANCE points can be regained during the course of the adventure, but your number of ENDURANCE points can never rise above the number you started with.

If you have successfully completed any of the previous adventures in the Lone Wolf series, you can carry your current scores of COMBAT SKILL and ENDURANCE points over to Book 10. You may also carry over any Weapons and Special Items you have in your possession at the end of your last adventure, and these should be entered on your new *Action Chart* (you are still limited to two Weapons and eight Backpack Items).

You may choose one bonus Magnakai Discipline to add to your *Action Chart* for every Lone Wolf Magnakai adventure you complete successfully (books 6–12).

MAGNAKAI DISCIPLINES

During your training as a Kai Lord, and in the course of the adventures that led to the discovery of *The Book of the Magnakai*, you have mastered all ten of the basic warrior skills known as the Kai Disciplines.

After studying *The Book of the Magnakai*, you have also reached the rank of Kai Master Superior, which means that you have learnt *three* of the Magnakai Disciplines listed below. It is up to you to choose which three skills these are. As all of the Magnakai Disciplines will be of use to you at some point on your adventure, pick your three with care. The correct use of a Magnakai Discipline at the right time can save your life.

The Magnakai skills are divided into groups, each of which is governed by a separate school of training. These groups are called 'Lore-circles'. By mastering all the Magnakai Disciplines in a particular Lore-circle, you can gain an increase in your COMBAT SKILL and ENDURANCE points score. (See the section 'Lore-circles of the Magnakai' for details of these bonuses.)

When you have chosen your three Magnakai Disciplines, enter them in the Magnakai Disciplines section of your *Action Chart*.

Weaponmastery

This Magnakai Discipline enables a Kai Master to become proficient in the use of all types of weapon. When you enter combat with a weapon you have mastered, you add 3 points to your COMBAT SKILL. The rank of Kai Master Superior, with which you begin the Magnakai series, means you are skilled in *three* of the weapons in the list below.

SPEAR

DAGGER

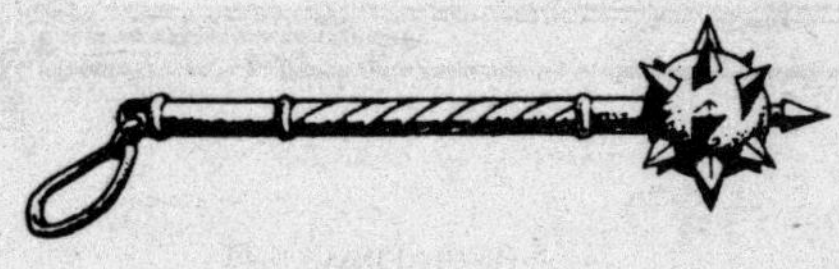

MACE

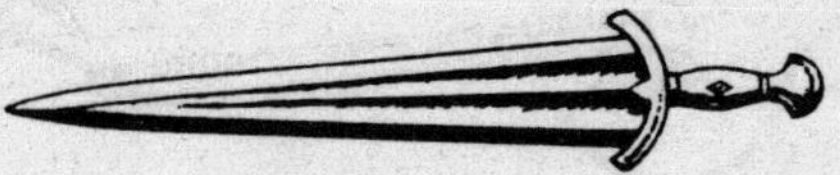

SHORT SWORD

WARHAMMER

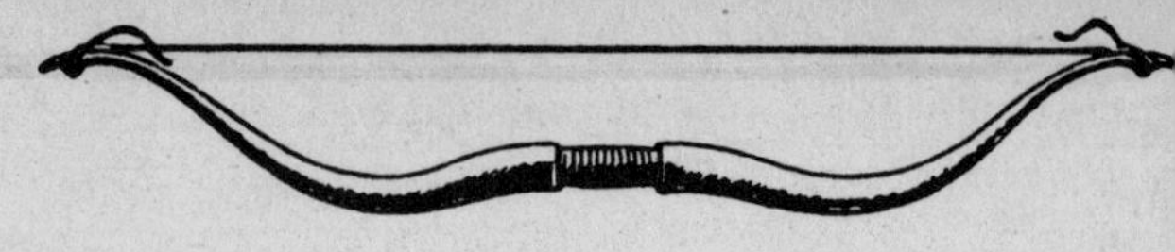

BOW

QUARTERSTAFF

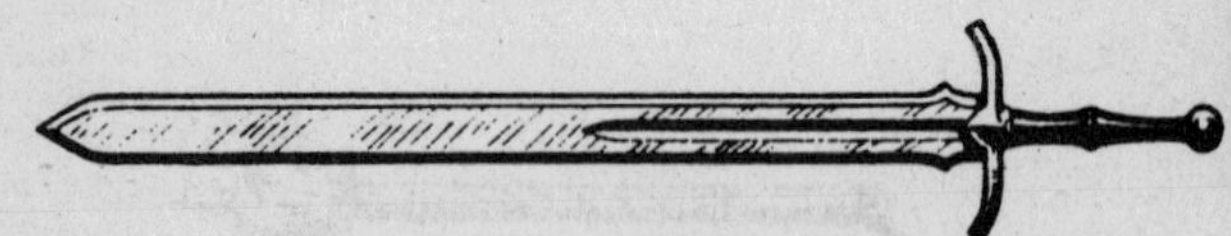

BROADSWORD

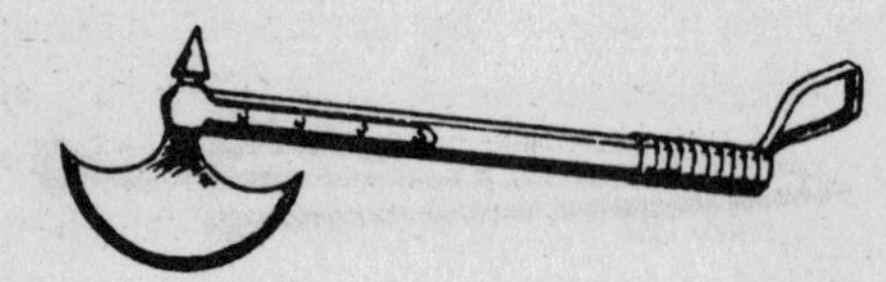

AXE

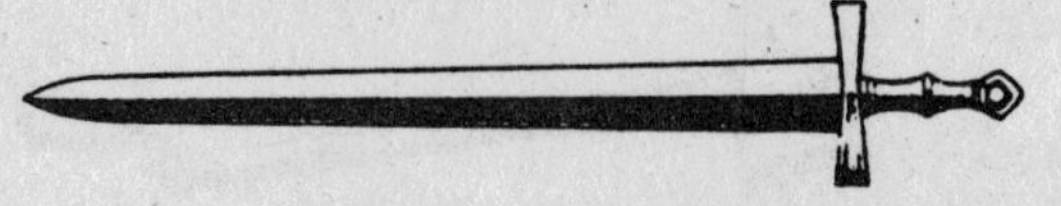

SWORD

If you choose this skill, write 'Weaponmastery: +3 COMBAT SKILL points' on your *Action Chart*, and tick your chosen weapons on the weapons list that appears on page 9. You cannot carry more than two weapons.

Animal Control
This Magnakai Discipline enables a Kai Master to communicate with most animals and to determine their purpose and intentions. It also enables a Kai Master to fight from the saddle with great advantage.

If you choose this skill, write 'Animal Control' on your *Action Chart*.

Curing
The possessor of this skill can restore 1 lost ENDURANCE point to his total for every numbered section of the book through which he passes, provided he is not involved in combat. (This can be done only after his ENDURANCE has fallen below its original level.) This Magnakai Discipline also enables a Kai Master to cure disease, blindness and any combat wounds sustained by others, as well as himself. Using the knowledge mastery of this skill provides will also allow a Kai Master to identify the properties of any herbs, roots and potions that may be encountered during the adventure.

If you choose this skill, write 'Curing: +1 ENDURANCE point for each section without combat' on your *Action Chart*.

Invisibility
This Magnakai skill allows a Kai Master to blend in with his surroundings, even in the most exposed terrain.

It will enable him to mask his body heat and scent, and to adopt the dialect and mannerisms of any town or city that he visits.

If you choose this skill, write 'Invisibility' on your *Action Chart*.

Huntmastery

This skill ensures that a Kai Master will never starve in the wild; he will always be able to hunt for food, even in areas of wasteland and desert. It also enables a Kai Master to move with great speed and dexterity and will allow him to ignore any extra loss of COMBAT SKILL points due to a surprise attack or ambush.

If you choose this skill, write 'Huntmastery' on your *Action Chart*.

Pathsmanship

In addition to the basic skill of being able to recognize the correct path in unknown territory, the Magnakai skill of Pathsmanship will enable a Kai Master to read foreign languages, decipher symbols, read footprints and tracks (even if they have been disturbed), and detect the presence of most traps. It also grants him the gift of always knowing intuitively the position of north.

If you choose this skill, write 'Pathsmanship' on your *Action Chart*.

Psi-surge

This psychic skill enables a Kai Master to attack an enemy using the force of his mind. It can be used as well as normal combat weapons and adds 4 extra points to your COMBAT SKILL.

It is a powerful Discipline, but it is also a costly one. For every round of combat in which you use Psi-surge, you must deduct 2 ENDURANCE points. A weaker form of Psi-surge called *Mindblast* can be used against an enemy without losing any ENDURANCE points, but it will add only 2 extra points to your COMBAT SKILL. Psi-surge cannot be used if your ENDURANCE falls to 6 points or below, and not all of the creatures encountered on your adventure will be affected by it; you will be told if a creature is immune.

If you choose this skill, write 'Psi-surge +4 COMBAT SKILL points but −2 ENDURANCE points per round' or 'Mindblast: +2 COMBAT SKILL points' on your *Action Chart*.

Psi-screen
Many of the hostile creatures that inhabit Magnamund have the ability to attack you using their Mindforce. The Magnakai Discipline of Psi-screen prevents you from losing any ENDURANCE points when subjected to this form of attack and greatly increases your defence against supernatural illusions and hypnosis.

If you choose this skill, write 'Psi-screen: no points lost when attacked by Mindforce' on your *Action Chart*.

Nexus
Mastery of this Magnakai skill will enable you to withstand extremes of heat and cold without losing ENDURANCE points, and to move items by your powers of concentration alone.

If you choose this skill, write 'Nexus' on your *Action Chart*.

Divination

This skill may warn a Kai Master of imminent or unseen danger, or enable him to detect an invisible or hidden enemy. It may also reveal the true purpose or intent of a stranger or strange object encountered in your adventure. Divination may enable you to communicate telepathically with another person and to sense if a creature possesses psychic abilities.

If you choose this skill, write 'Divination' on your *Action Chart*.

If you successfully complete the mission as set in Book 10 of the Lone Wolf Magnakai series, you may add a further Magnakai Discipline of your choice to your *Action Chart* in Book 11. This additional skill, together with your other Magnakai skills and any Special Items that you have found and been able to keep during your adventures, may then be used in the next adventure, which is called *THE PRISONERS OF TIME*.

EQUIPMENT

Before you leave Anari and journey across Magnamund to the principality of Eru, the Elder Magi give you a map of Ghatan and its surrounding territories (see the inside front cover of this book), and a pouch of gold. To find out how much gold is in the pouch, pick a number from the *Random Number Table*. Add 10 to the number you have picked. The total equals the number of Gold Crowns inside the pouch, and you should now enter this number in the 'Gold Crowns' section of your *Action Chart*. If you have successfully completed books 1–9 of the Lone Wolf adventures, you may add this sum to the total sum of Crowns you already possess. You can carry a maximum of only fifty Crowns, but additional Crowns can be left in safe-keeping at your Kai monastery.

The Senate of Tahou, in gratitude for your help in saving their city from destruction, offer you a choice of equipment to aid you on your perilous mission. You can take five items from the list below, again adding to these, if necessary, any you may already possess. However, remember that you can carry a maximum of two Weapons and eight Backpack Items.

SWORD (Weapons)
BOW (Weapons)
QUIVER (Special Items) This contains six arrows. Tick them off as they are used.

ROPE (Backpack Items)

POTION OF LAUMSPUR (Backpack Items) This potion restores 4 ENDURANCE points to your total when swallowed after combat. There is enough for only one dose.

LANTERN (Backpack Items)

MACE (Weapons)

3 MEALS (Meals) Each Meal takes up one space in your Backpack.

DAGGER (Weapons)

List the five items that you choose on your *Action Chart*, under the heading given in brackets, and make a note of any effect they may have on your ENDURANCE points or COMBAT SKILL.

How to carry equipment

Now that you have your equipment, the following list shows you how it is carried. You do not need to make notes but you can refer back to this list in the course of your adventure.

SWORD – carried in the hand.
BOW – carried in the hand.
QUIVER – slung over your shoulder.
ROPE – carried in the Backpack.
POTION OF LAUMSPUR – carried in the Backpack.
LANTERN – carried in the Backpack.
MACE – carried in the hand.
MEALS – carried in the Backpack.
DAGGER – carried in the hand.

How much can you carry?

Weapons
The maximum number of weapons that you may carry is *two*.

Backpack Items
These must be stored in your Backpack. Because space is limited, you may keep a maximum of only eight articles, including Meals, in your Backpack at any one time.

Special Items
Special Items are not carried in the Backpack. When you discover a Special Item, you will be told how to carry it.

The maximum number of Special Items that can be carried on any adventure is twelve. Surplus Special Items may be left for safe-keeping at your Kai monastery.

Gold Crowns
These are always carried in the Belt Pouch. It will hold a maximum of fifty Crowns.

Food
Food is carried in your Backpack. Each Meal counts as one item.

Any item that may be of use and can be picked up on your adventure and entered on your *Action Chart* is given initial capitals (eg Gold Dagger, Magic Pendant) in the text. Unless you are told it is a Special Item, carry it in your Backpack.

How to use your equipment

Weapons
Weapons aid you in combat. If you have the Magnakai Discipline of Weaponmastery and a correct weapon, it adds 3 points to your COMBAT SKILL. If you enter a combat with no weapons, deduct 4 points from your COMBAT SKILL and fight with your bare hands. If you find a weapon during the adventure, you may pick it up and use it. (Remember that you can only carry *two* weapons at once.)

Bow and Arrows

During your adventure there will be opportunities to use a bow and arrow. If you equip yourself with this weapon, and you possess at least one arrow, you may use it when the text of a particular section allows you to do so. The bow is a useful weapon as it enables you to hit an enemy at a distance. However, a bow cannot be used in hand-to-hand combat, and it is therefore strongly recommended that you also equip yourself with a close combat weapon, such as a sword or mace.

In order to use a bow you must possess a quiver and at least one arrow. Each time the bow is used, erase an arrow from your *Action Chart*. A bow cannot, of course, be used if you exhaust your supply of arrows, but the opportunity may arise during your adventure for you to replenish your stock of arrows.

If you have the Magnakai Discipline of Weaponmastery with a bow, you may add 3 to any number that you pick from the *Random Number Table*, when using the bow. If you enter combat armed only with a bow, you must deduct 4 points from your COMBAT SKILL and fight with your bare hands.

Backpack Items

During your travels you will discover various useful items which you may wish to keep. (Remember that you can carry a maximum of eight items in your Backpack at any time.) You may exchange or discard them at any point when you are not involved in combat.

Special Items

Special Items are not carried in the Backpack. When

you discover a Special Item, you will be told how to carry it. If you have successfully completed previous Lone Wolf books, you may already possess Special Items.

The maximum number of Special Items that a Kai Master can carry during an adventure is twelve. Surplus Special Items may be left in safe keeping at your Kai monastery.

Gold Crowns
The currency of Eru is the Lune, but Gold Crowns are readily accepted at an exchange rate of 4 Lune for every 1 Gold Crown.

Food
You will need to eat regularly during your adventure. If you do not have any food when you are instructed to eat a Meal, you will lose 3 ENDURANCE points. If you have chosen the Magnakai Discipline of Huntmastery as one of your skills, you will not need to tick off a Meal when instructed to eat.

Potion of Laumspur
This is a healing potion that can restore 4 ENDURANCE points to your total when swallowed after combat. There is enough for one dose only. If you discover any other potion during the adventure, you will be informed of its effect. All potions are Backpack Items.

There will be occasions during your adventure when you have to fight an enemy. The enemy's COMBAT SKILL and ENDURANCE points are given in the text. Lone Wolf's aim in the combat is to kill the enemy by reducing his ENDURANCE points to zero while losing as few ENDURANCE points as possible himself.

At the start of a combat, enter Lone Wolf's and the enemy's ENDURANCE points in the appropriate boxes on the Combat Record section of your *Action Chart*.

The sequence for combat is as follows:

1. Add any extra points gained through your Magnakai Disciplines and Special Items to your current COMBAT SKILL total.
2. Subtract the COMBAT SKILL of your enemy from this total. The result is your *Combat Ratio*. Enter it on the *Action Chart*.

Example
Lone Wolf (COMBAT SKILL 15) is attacked by a Nightstalker (COMBAT SKILL 22). He is not given the opportunity to evade combat, but must stand and fight as the creature leaps on him. Lone Wolf has the Magnakai Discipline of Psi-surge to which the Nightstalker is not immune, so Lone Wolf adds 4 points to his COMBAT SKILL giving him a total COMBAT SKILL of 19.

He subtracts the Nightstalker's COMBAT SKILL from his own, giving a *Combat Ratio* of −3. (19 − 22 = −3). −3 is noted on the *Action Chart* as the *Combat Ratio*.

3. When you have your *Combat Ratio*, pick a number from the *Random Number Table*.

4. Turn to the *Combat Results Table* on the inside back cover of the book. Along the top of the chart are shown the *Combat Ratio* numbers. Find the number that is the same as your *Combat Ratio* and cross-reference it with the random number that you have picked (the random numbers appear on the side of the chart). You now have the number of ENDURANCE points lost by both Lone Wolf and his enemy in this round of combat. (*E* represents points lost by the enemy; *LW* represents points lost by Lone Wolf.)

   Example
   The *Combat Ratio* between Lone Wolf and the Nightstalker has been established as −3. If the number picked from the *Random Number Table* is a 6, then the result of the first round of combat is:

   Lone Wolf loses 3 ENDURANCE points (plus an additional 2 points for using Psi-surge).
   Nightstalker loses 6 ENDURANCE points.

5. On the *Action Chart*, mark the changes in ENDURANCE points to the participants in the combat.

6. Unless otherwise instructed, or unless you have an option to evade, the next round of combat now starts.

7. Repeat the sequence from stage 3.

This process of combat continues until ENDURANCE points of either the enemy or Lone Wolf are reduced to zero, at which point the one with the zero score is declared dead. If Lone Wolf is dead, the adventure is over. If the enemy is dead, Lone Wolf proceeds but with his ENDURANCE points reduced.

A summary of Combat Rules appears on the page after the *Random Number Table*.

Evasion of combat

During your adventure you may be given the chance to evade combat. If you have already engaged in a round of combat and decide to evade, calculate the combat for that round in the usual manner. All points lost by the enemy as a result of that round are ignored, and you make your escape. Only Lone Wolf may lose ENDURANCE points during that round, but then that is the risk of running away! You may evade only if the text of the particular section allows you to do so.

LEVELS OF MAGNAKAI TRAINING

The following table is a guide to the rank and titles that are achieved by Kai Masters at each stage of their training. As you successfully complete each adventure in the Lone Wolf Magnakai series, you will gain an additional Magnakai Discipline and progress towards the ultimate distinction of a Kai Warrior – Kai Grand Mastership.

No. of Magnakai Disciplines mastered by Kai Master	*Magnakai Rank*
1	Kai Master
2	Kai Master Senior
3	Kai Master Superior – *You begin the Lone Wolf Magnakai adventures with this level of training*
4	Primate
5	Tutelary
6	Principalin
7	Mentora
8	Scion-kai
9	Archmaster
10	Kai Grand Master

LORE-CIRCLES OF THE MAGNAKAI

In the years before their massacre, the Kai Masters of Sommerlund devoted themselves to the study of the Magnakai. These skills were divided into four schools of training called 'Lore-circles'. By mastering all of the Magnakai Disciplines of a Lore-circle, the Kai Masters developed their fighting prowess (COMBAT SKILL), and their physical and mental stamina (ENDURANCE) to a level far higher than any mortal warrior could otherwise attain.

Listed below are the four Lore-circles of the Magnakai and the skills that must be mastered in order to complete them.

Title of Magnakai Lore-circle	*Magnakai Disciplines needed to complete the Lore-circle*
CIRCLE OF FIRE	Weaponmastery & Huntmastery
CIRCLE OF LIGHT	Animal control & Curing
CIRCLE OF SOLARIS	Invisibility, Huntmastery & Pathsmanship
CIRCLE OF THE SPIRIT	Psi-surge, Psi-shield, Nexus & Divination

By completing a Lore-circle, you may add to your COMBAT SKILL and ENDURANCE the extra bonus points that are shown below.

Lore-circle bonuses

	COMBAT SKILL	ENDURANCE
CIRCLE OF FIRE	+1	+2
CIRCLE OF LIGHT	0	+3
CIRCLE OF SOLARIS	+1	+3
CIRCLE OF THE SPIRIT	+3	+3

All bonus points that you acquire by completing a Lore-circle are additions to your basic COMBAT SKILL and ENDURANCE scores.

IMPROVED DISCIPLINES

As you rise through the higher levels of Magnakai training you will find that your skills will steadily improve. If you are a Kai Master that has reached the rank of Primate (four skills), Tutelary (five skills), Principalin (six skills), or Mentora (seven skills), you will now benefit from the improvements to the following Magnakai Disciplines:

PRIMATE

Animal Control
Primates with this Magnakai Discipline are able to repel an animal that is intent on harming them by blocking

its sense of taste and smell. The level of success is dependent on the size and ferocity of the animal.

Curing

Primates with this skill have the ability to delay the effect of any poisons, including venoms, that they may come into contact with. Although a Kai Primate with this skill is not able to neutralize a poison, he is able to slow its effect, giving him more time to find an antidote or cure.

Huntmastery

Primates with this skill have greatly increased agility and are able to climb without the use of climbing aids, such as ropes, etc.

Psi-surge

Primates with the Magnakai Discipline of Psi-surge can, by concentrating their psychic powers upon an object, set up vibrations that may lead to the disruption or destruction of the object.

Nexus

Primates with the skill of Nexus are able to offer a far greater resistance than before to the effects of noxious gases and fumes.

TUTELARY

Weaponmastery

Tutelaries are able to use defensive combat skills to great effect when fighting unarmed. When entering combat without a weapon, Tutelaries lose only 2 points from their COMBAT SKILL, instead of 4 points.

Invisibility
Tutelaries are able to increase the effectiveness of their skill when hiding from an enemy by drawing the enemy's attention to a place other than that in which they are hiding. The effectiveness of this ability increases as a Kai Master rises in rank.

Pathsmanship
Tutelaries with this skill can detect an enemy ambush within 500 yards of their position unless their ENDURANCE level is low due to a large number of wounds sustained or to lack of food.

Psi-screen
Tutelaries with this skill develop mental defences against magical charms and hostile telepathy. The effectiveness of this ability increases in strength as a Kai Master rises in rank.

Divination
Tutelaries who possess this Magnakai Discipline are able to recognize objects or creatures with magical skills or abilities. However, this improved Discipline can be negated if the creature or object is shielded from detection.

PRINCIPALIN

Animal Control
Principalins with this skill are able to call on a woodland animal (if nearby) to aid them, either in combat, or to act as a messenger or guide. The number of animals that can be summoned increases as a Kai Master rises in rank.

Invisibility
Principalins are able to mask any sounds made by their movements while using this skill.

Huntmastery
Principalins with this Magnakai Discipline are able to intensify their eyesight at will, giving them telescopic vision.

Psi-surge
Principalins using this skill in combat are able to confuse an enemy by planting seeds of doubt in its mind. The effectiveness of this ability increases as a Kai Master rises in rank.

Nexus
Principalins with this ability can extinguish fires by force of will alone. The size of the fire, and the number that can be extinguished using Nexus increases as a Kai Master rises in rank.

MENTORA

Weaponmastery
Mentoras skilled in Weaponmastery are more accurate when using all missile weapons, whether fired (eg, a bow) or thrown (eg, a dagger). When using a bow or thrown weapon and instructed to pick a number from the *Random Number Table*, add 2 to the number picked if you are a Mentora with the Magnakai Discipline of Weaponmastery.

Curing
Mentoras with this skill are able to neutralize the effects of any poisons, venoms or toxins with which they come into contact.

Pathsmanship
Mentoras who possess this Magnakai Discipline are able to cross any kind of terrain on foot without leaving any tracks, even if the ground is covered in snow.

Psi-screen
Mentoras with this ability can protect themselves from evil spirits and other non-corporeal beings that attack with psychic energy. The effectiveness of this ability increases as a Kai Master rises in rank.

Divination
Mentoras who possess this skill are able to detect psychic residues lingering in a place where a dramatic event, such as a battle, a murder, a ritual sacrifice or a ritual ceremony, has taken place. By meditating at the scene of the incident, a Kai Mentora is able to visualize the event, even though it may have occurred in the distant past.

The nature of any additional improvements and how they affect your Magnakai Disciplines will be noted in the Improved Disciplines section of future Lone Wolf books.

MAGNAKAI WISDOM

Your quest to retrieve the last three Lorestones of Nyxator from the clutches of the Darklords will be fraught with deadly dangers. The evil host of Helgedad will summon their most brutal forces to thwart your Magnakai quest. Make notes as you progress through this story – they will be of great help in this and in future adventures.

Many things that you find will help you during your mission. Some Special Items will be of use in this and future Lone Wolf books, while others may be red herrings of no real value at all, so be selective in what you decide to keep.

Choose your three Magnakai Disciplines with care, for a wise choice enables any player to complete the quest, no matter how weak their initial COMBAT SKILL and ENDURANCE points scores. Successful completion of previous Lone Wolf adventures, although an advantage, is not essential for the completion of this Magnakai adventure.

The restoration of the Kai and the future of your homeland depends on the success of this mission. May the spirit of your ancestors and the wisdom of the great God Kai guide you on the path of the Magnakai.

Good luck!

1

It is dawn on mid-summer's day when you ride out of Tahou. Since your victory over Zakhan Kimah, your appearance in a public place has been enough to provoke spontaneous cheering from the Tahouese, who regard you as their saviour. But on this warm, sunny morning you leave the city unnoticed, for on this occasion you appear to be just another messenger.

The army uniform you wear and the white horse you ride are part of an elaborate deception conceived by the Elder Magi. In order to make Darklord Gnaag believe that you are returning to Sommerlund, you have given your Kai cloak and tunic to your friend Banedon. Disguised as you, he will leave for Sommerlund aboard his flying ship *Skyrider* this afternoon. A formal ceremony is planned to mark his departure and another awaits his arrival at the King's Citadel in Holmgard. Gnaag has vowed to kill you: it is a vow which has become an obsession that torments him like a poisoned wound. It is hoped that Banedon's much-publicized flight home will lure Gnaag's vengeful eyes away to the north and raise your chances of success at Torgar considerably.

1

Your ride ends in Firina, where you catch a barge down-river to the port of Talon. There you hear news of a rebellion in Barrakeesh, the Vassagonian capital, and reports of the sudden withdrawal of all Vassagonia's troops from the lands she invaded early in the war. It bodes well for the continuing struggle against the Darklords, for Vassagonia was their only major ally. You spend one night in Talon before buying passage aboard a merchantman on its way along the Tentarias, and five days later you disembark at Garthen, the capital of Talestria.

Talestria was overrun in the early days of the war but the neighbouring country of Palmyrion came quickly to her aid. The armies of Talestria and Palmyrion united and fought the invading horde, led by Warlord Zegron of Ogia, on the battle-plains to the north of Garthen. For three days and three nights a bitter struggle raged and the allies were sorely pressed to withstand the overwhelming numbers of the enemy ranged against them. But on the morning of the fourth day, the unexpected arrival of the dwarven army of Bor was to seal Zegron's doom. His mighty force crumbled and the survivors, fleeing northwards in chaos, were pursued relentlessly. The latest news tells of the allies' capture of Xanar, a major Ogian stronghold, and their continued advance westward along the Blackshroud Trail.

The Royal Court of Queen Evaine would be honoured to assist you, but secrecy is paramount to the success of your quest and so you shun the Royal Palace and take lodgings instead at a humble dockside tavern. There you arrange transportation to Eru aboard a brigantine bound for Humbold, the Eruan capital, and leave next day on the noon tide. Upon your arrival, you make your way to the city's ancient quarter where the Elder Magi have arranged a clandestine meeting with Prince Graygor. In the cellar of a disused warehouse, the young Prince waits patiently for your coming. Like you, he is dressed in the clothes of a messenger in order that he can walk the streets of his city incognito. He welcomes you with a salute, bringing his hand diagonally across his chest, and assures you that your true identity is known only to him. For over an hour you discuss your plans and listen to the Prince recount some of the events that have disturbed the peace of Eru. Two years ago, Drakkarim renegades from the Hammerlands attacked and overran his northern city of Luomi. The inhabitants were slaughtered and the holy temple of Luomi, around which the city was founded, was looted and burnt to the ground. Only recently did he learn from the Elder Magi that the ancient temple held the Lorestone of Luomi, one of the three Lorestones now locked in Torgar. At the time of the attack the Prince's army was too small to repel the invaders and he was forced to abandon the city, as well as the border town of Cetza. But in the past month he has joined forces with King Sarnac of Lencia, and together they have recaptured Luomi and driven Baron Shinzar and his Hammerland rebels all the way back to Cetza, within thirty miles of the border.

The prince invites you to accompany him to Luomi where he is to resume command of his army and lead them to battle. He provides you with a fine Eruan steed and a new disguise that will enable you to travel through Eru without drawing undue attention to yourself.

1

Dressed as an Eruan Pathfinder, one of an elite unit of woodsmen who operate in the harsh territories bordering the Hellswamp, you ride north with the Prince's entourage and arrive at the city five days later. Every house, stable, tavern and municipal building is filled to overflowing with knights and men at arms. But, despite their cramped billets and meagre rations, the soldiers of Eru and Lencia are in good spirits, for tomorrow they march against a foe they have already beaten in battle, and most are eager to finish the job once and for all. You are given lodgings within the main citadel of Luomi and later that evening, after the prince has attended a war conference with King Sarnac, you meet in private to discuss the next stage of your quest.

'There are two ways to reach Torgar,' says the Prince, as you study the map given to you by the Senate of Tahou. 'You can cross the River Brol and make your way northwards through the Moggador Forest, or you can go to Pirsi and seek out Sebb Jarel. He is the leader of a brave band of partisans who have ambushed and resisted the Drakkarim ever since they invaded. If there is a path to Torgar between the Hellswamp and the Isle of Ghosts, he will know it.'

You ponder the choices and wonder why the Prince has not suggested the simplest route of all: north across the Isle of Ghosts. When you mention this he shakes his head ominously. 'The isle is cursed,' he says, pointing at the map with an accusing finger. 'Few have ever come out of that dreadful place alive. And of those poor wretches who have survived, only one has kept a grip of his sanity. His name is Sebb Jarel.'

Next day you rise with the dawn and prepare to set off on your journey to Torgar. There are two routes open to you: you can ride to Pirsi and seek out Sebb Jarel, the partisan leader, and the only man who can guide you through this treacherous wilderness; or you can accompany Prince Graygor to battle at Cetza. If his army beats the Drakkarim and forces them to retreat, the way across the River Brol will be open and you will be able to approach Torgar under cover of the Moggador Forest. Consult the map at the front of the book before you decide which route to take.

If you wish to go to Pirsi, turn to **176**.

If you choose to accompany Prince Graygor to battle at Cetza, turn to **308**.

2

Using your mastery of Nexus you extinguish the flames that are scorching your arm, and immediately set about helping those Palmyrions who have survived the devastating attack. Less than half are able to stand, but you manage to pull them into a defensive circle in time to fight the Drakkarim who are charging along the street.

Drakkarim Garrison:
COMBAT SKILL 26 ENDURANCE 39

If you win the combat, turn to **332**.

3

Fear returns to tie a knot in your stomach as you detect the scent of live Akataz. Instinctively you flatten yourself to the ground and a twisting grey blur arcs over your head and crashes headlong into the undergrowth. You are unharmed but you sense that the dog is just the first of many that are rushing towards this part of the forest, drawn by the blood of their kin and the scent of your body. Before it can recover from its failed attack, you jump to your feet and sprint away.

Turn to **31**.

4

An hour before dawn, you leave Cetza and ride across the open grasslands that slope gently towards the River Brol. A full moon and the gathering light of day help you identify the landmarks that Prince Graygor told you to look out for to help guide you to a ford close to the site of an abandoned copper mine. His directions prove accurate and by mid-morning you find yourself on a ridge that overlooks the ford and its cluster of derelict mining huts.

If you have the Magnakai Discipline of Huntmastery and have reached the Kai rank of Principalin or more, turn to **324**.

If you have the Magnakai Discipline of Pathsmanship and have reached the Kai rank of Tutelary or more, turn to **241**.

If you do not possess either of these skills, or have yet to reach these levels of Kai training, turn to **108**.

5

You notice there is a spot where a gantry passes directly over the ball of green flame. If you could crawl to that spot you would be able to cup your hands below the Lorestones. Paido could then destroy the crystal rods, and the Lorestones, freed of the energy beams, would drop into your hands.

It is a bold plan but you feel confident that it will succeed.

Turn to **40**.

6 – *Illustration I (overleaf)*

You share the officer's horse as he leads his company back along a route they have already ridden. Steadily the road winds upwards through the hills towards a ridge of yellow rock and, as you reach the crest of the ridge, you catch your first awe-inspiring glimpse of Torgar.

The walls of this grim city-fortress stand upon the brink of a ravine cut deep by centuries of rushing water. A natural causeway of stone spans this dark chasm and provides the only means of approaching Torgar from the south. Its position and its defences seem impregnable. It commands the only road into the barren land of Ghatan, and any who dare travel that road must pass over the causeway and through the city's great iron gate.

I. The grim city-fortress of Torgar

In the past there have been few who would venture willingly to Torgar, but now the causeway and its approaches swarm with such men. They are the soldiers of Talestria and Palmyrion, and they have come with their engines of war to lay siege to this grim Drakkar fortress.

The scout officer spurs his horse away from the ridge and you are carried towards a cluster of tents that stand on high ground overlooking the siege-works. As you arrive, a group of knights steps forward to take the horse's reins. You dismount with the officer and follow as he enters the largest tent.

If you have ever visited the land of Talestria in a previous Lone Wolf adventure, turn to **45**.
If not, turn to **346**.

7

The captain grunts his approval and returns your salute. Then he catches sight of your signet ring and suddenly his mood becomes much more friendly. He orders the townsfolk to lower their pistols and return to their homes and begrudgingly they obey his command. 'Come,' he says, placing his hand on your shoulder. 'You must be thirsty after your day's ride.'

He pushes open the tavern door and draws aside a tattered leather curtain. A dozen pairs of eyes look towards you as you enter, stare briefly, then return to their own business.

'I see you come to Pirsi with the Prince's favour,' says the captain, casting a glance at the ring you wear as you raise the tankard of ale he places before you. 'What news do you bring from the Royal Court?'

'I'm here on a mission, a secret mission of great importance,' you reply, guardedly. 'I must speak with Seb Jarel, for only he can help me accomplish the task. I am at liberty to say no more.'

The captain looks at you quizzically. 'It's unlike Prince Graygor to entrust such responsibility to one of your rank, soldier. If you expect me to take you to Jarel you have first to satisfy me that you're a Pathfinder. That bandit Baron Shinzar has sent men to find Jarel before – on missions of assassination. I want proof you're not another one of his agents.'

He peers over your shoulder towards the tavern bar and signals to the owner by blinking three times. The metallic click of a crossbow being cocked and your Kai sixth sense alert you to the weapon that is now pointed at your back. 'Tell me, soldier, where were you trained as a Pathfinder? Was it in Humbold, in Sharwhan, or in Testla?'

If you have completed the Lore-circle of the Spirit, turn to **46**.
If you do not have mastery of this Lore-circle you must hazard a guess at the answer.
If you answer, 'Humbold', turn to **111**.
If you answer, 'Sharwhan', turn to **287**.
If you answer, 'Testla', turn to **152**.

8

You spur your horse down the slope and gallop along an overgrown track that leads to the ford. The log huts are shrouded in silence, but as you draw level with them, a gruff shout shatters this illusion of peacefulness and a hail of arrows cuts through the air.

One of the black shafts buries itself in your horse's neck. He shrieks in pain and crashes to his knees, hurling you into the river. You gulp a mouthful of the icy water and struggle to your feet, coughing and cursing, just in time to see your ambushers pour out of the nearest hut and advance towards you. Some are reloading their bows as they run.

If you have a bow and wish to use it, turn to **131**.
If you wish to try to escape by wading across the ford, turn to **166**.
If you wish to draw a hand weapon and prepare for combat, turn to **251**.

9

Your shaft arcs towards the Baron, but it reaches him just as he turns to push his troops into line and it glances off his pauldron, a shaped steel shoulder guard bolted to his breastplate. Alerted to your presence, he spins around and glares into your eyes, his red axe glinting as sunlight breaks through the haze of battle smoke.

If you possess the Sommerswerd, turn to **113**.
If you do not possess this Special Item, turn to **126**.

10

An evil smile spreads across Roark's face as the Demonlord finally comes to his aid. You strike the creature but your blows merely splinter your weapon. Incensed by your defiance, Tagazin leaps upon you and sinks his fangs deep into your chest. Pain explodes through your body but the agony is soon obliterated by the numbing chill of death.

Your life and your quest end here.

11

Beaten and bloodied, the surviving Krorn back away whimpering as you climb over the bodies of their slain brothers and stalk towards them. Baron Shinzar screams in anger and lifts his axe high. He barges through his misshapen troops and stands before you, glaring like a man possessed. 'Meet your doom, Eruan scum!' he sneers, and strikes out at your head. You block the blow but your weapon is destroyed in a flash of sparks (delete this weapon from your *Action Chart*): the Baron wields a weapon forged by sorcery. As he lifts it anew, you prepare to dodge its lethal caress.

Pick a number from the *Random Number Table*. If you have the Magnakai Discipline of Huntmastery, add 2 to the number you have picked.

If your total is now *0–3*, turn to **310**.
If it is 4 or more, turn to **229**.

12

Using your ability to intensify your vision you focus on the advancing horsemen. You see that they are all wearing surcoats of scarlet and grey, embroidered with a crest bearing an open hand. The only horsemen who wear this livery are the cavalry of Talestria.

If you wish to wave down these riders, turn to **61**.
If you would rather hide from them beneath the bridge, turn to **322**.

13

Drawing on your Kai skills you blend with the shadows and stand absolutely still. The Death Knight warrior appears, filling the archway with his massive frame. He snatches up the spear in his mailed fist, turns, and then hauls himself out of the ditch, grunting and cursing his carelessness as he struggles in his heavy armour.

You wait for about twenty minutes before leaving your hiding place and working your way along the ditch.

Turn to **124**.

14

You focus your Kai skill on Adamas's hand but you cannot tell which side of the coin is showing. All you can detect is a strong magical aura, indicating that the coin is magically shielded. You have no option but to guess which side is showing.

If you wish to call 'heads', turn to **330**.
If you wish to call 'tails', turn to **212**.

15

You land with a crash among the roots and briars, and roll to lessen the shock of impact. Sharp thorns graze your hands and knees (lose 1 ENDURANCE point) but otherwise you survive the jump intact. Quickly you gather up your equipment and press on into the eerie forest.

Turn to **50**.

16

A narrow pathway branches away from the main alley and you rush along it, barging aside a Hammerlander who appears suddenly from a doorway. The screams of your company and the clash of swords echo in the narrow confines of the passage as you make your escape swiftly towards the centre of the town. The passage opens on to a wider street where a barn-like building stands at the corner. Crouching at a window on the upper floor is a Drakkarim archer with an arrow notched ready to fire. He sees you appear and releases his straining bowstring, sending his arrow whistling towards your heart.

Pick a number from the *Random Number Table*. If you have the Magnakai Discipline of Huntmastery, add 3 to the number you have picked.

If the total is now *0–2*, turn to **264**.
If it is *3–5*, turn to **121**.
If it is *6* or more, turn to **319**.

17

'Naog daka!' snarls a voice in the corridor behind. You spin round to see two Drakkarim warriors, both armed with loaded crossbows. Slowly you let your hand drift towards your weapon but your move does not go unnoticed. Suddenly a starburst of pain explodes in your head and darkness washes over your vision as you are slammed back against the door by the force of the bolt which has penetrated your skull. Death is instantaneous.

Your life and your quest end here.

18

You coax your horse along the rocky trail as it winds its way upstream towards the foothills of the Eru Range. By early evening you have traversed several miles of difficult terrain and, by chance, you find yourself at the entrance to an incredible gorge. It is filled with a sea of wild flowers so colourful that you are dazzled by their brilliance. The scent they exude is extremely potent and you feel a tremendous urge to dismount and lie down to sleep among the beautiful blooms.

If you have the Magnakai Discipline of Nexus and have reached the rank of Primate or more, turn to **83**.

If you have the Magnakai Discipline of Curing, turn to **255**.

If you possess neither of these skills, turn to **167**.

19

It becomes colder as night draws its black cloak around the clearing. Having done without sleep the previous evening you are now very tired, and settle down to rest with your back against the mossy temple wall. You are just drifting off when you become aware that something is moving near the edge of the trees.

Shadowy shapes wreathed in mist are swirling around the pines like phantoms in a dream.

If you have the Magnakai Discipline of Psi-screen and have reached the Kai rank of Mentora, turn to **93**.

If you do not possess this skill or have yet to reach this level of Kai training, turn to **228**.

20

Tagazin shudders as the blows of the Sommerswerd rob him of his supernatural strength. His body becomes pale, almost transparent, and tiny tendrils of smoke curl from his skin as if his body was slowly evaporating. He retreats towards the centre of the temple and leaps on to the marble block. There is a chilling howl and suddenly the shadowy chamber is flooded with a blinding light. Thunder booms and the walls shake. Terrified, Roark and his companions flee through the shattered doors and scramble up the stairs. Crackling bolts of white lightning leap from the marble block to tear great chunks of rock from the walls, and the air seethes with a cloying stench that threatens to suffocate you. With terror in your heart you bound up the stairs and escape as the defeated spirit of the Demonlord vents its spite on the chamber below.

Turn to **341**.

21

You reach the King's headquarters only to discover that he is not there: he has taken personal command of his Horse Knights and mounted men-at-arms, and led them in an attack on the enemy's reinforcements. From the top of the hill you can see a huge cavalry battle taking place on the grasslands south of Cetza. Amid the wheeling ranks of armoured horsemen, at the very heart of the fiercest fighting, flies the King's banner. It would be impossible for you to reach him and request that he save the Prince.

Mindful of the time that has been lost, you turn your horse about and set off towards the Prince's reserves, determined now to lead them yourself.

Turn to **49**.

22

Your Kai skill warns you that the robed figures possess magical abilities. The glass globes they are holding contain a volatile mixture of phosphorous and oil. If the globes were to break, the contents would burst into flames immediately on contact with the air.

If you have a bow and wish to fire an arrow at one of the globes, turn to **293**.
If not, turn to **199**.

23

You fling aside the curtain and rush through the archway into the passage beyond. The two cave guards turn to face you but the speed of your escape leaves them fumbling for their spears. You reach the exit, breathless and fearful, and catch sight of a patrol of horsemen arriving at the camp. They dismount, tether their horses to some bushes and make their way wearily towards the main campfire. Seeing an opportunity to escape, you rush to the first bush and snatch up the reins of the nearest mount. Suddenly a cry echoes from the cave mouth: the guards are raising the alarm. You climb into the saddle but your escape is blocked by a partisan horseman riding up the narrow track that leads into the camp.

Partisan Horseman:
COMBAT SKILL 17 ENDURANCE 24

If you win the combat, turn to **239**.

24

Gradually your Psi-screen weakens enough to enable the phantoms to engulf you with their snaky tendrils. You shudder with fear as they coil around your limbs, filling them with a terrible chill that steals your strength and your will to resist. Reluctantly you surrender to their numbing caress and slip into a sleep from which there will be no awakening.

Your life and your quest end here.

25

You rub your eyes and look around you at a campsite

nestling in a hollow at the foot of a great, snow-capped mountain. It is occupied by a host of partisans, who are busy tending their ponies and sharpening weapons dulled by heavy fighting. Your escort helps you to dismount and you are led through the camp to a cave hidden beneath a huge outcrop of rock. As you enter the cave and follow a torchlit passage, you hear voices echoing in the distance and your keen nostrils catch the scent of roasting meat. The passage ends at a curtained archway guarded by two men with spears. They look at you brusquely, as if you were a stray dog, but your escort explains your purpose here and they stand aside to allow you an audience with their leader, Sebb Jarel.

Turn to **38**.

26

A wave of pain begins to envelop your mind, but your psychic defences deflect the attack before it overwhelms your senses: lose 1 ENDURANCE point.

The attack ceases but your fear grows as you watch the jackal-like Demonlord leap from the marble block and come bounding towards the door.

If you have a bow and wish to use it, turn to **147**.
If not, turn to **174**.

27

Your pack and weapons land safely among the tangle of foliage that carpets the ground on the opposite side of the chasm. Free of their encumbrance, you take a long run-up and leap feet-first across the gap.

Pick a number from the *Random Number Table*. If you have the Magnakai Discipline of Huntmastery, add 3 to the number you have picked.

If your total is now *0–3*, turn to **54**.
If it is *4* or more, turn to **15**.

28 – *Illustration II*

Suddenly a dozen webbed hands slap over the sides of the boat and six ghoulish, dome-shaped heads rise from the river. Their mottled throat sacs puff and slacken fitfully as these creatures clamber over the gunwales and launch their attack.

Ciquali: COMBAT SKILL 29   ENDURANCE 36

Unless you possess the Magnakai Discipline of Huntmastery, reduce your COMBAT SKILL by 3 points for the first round of combat due to the surprise of the attack.

If you win and the fight lasts four rounds or less, turn to **169**.
If you win and the fight lasts longer than four rounds, turn to **309**.

29

On your return to Prince Graygor's tent you are shown to your sleeping area by one of his heralds. It is little more than a pile of straw strewn on the bare ground, but you have slept in worse places than this and you are now too exhausted to complain or look for somewhere more suitable to rest.

Unless you possess a blanket, lose 1 ENDURANCE point due to an uncomfortable night's sleep.

Turn to **280**.

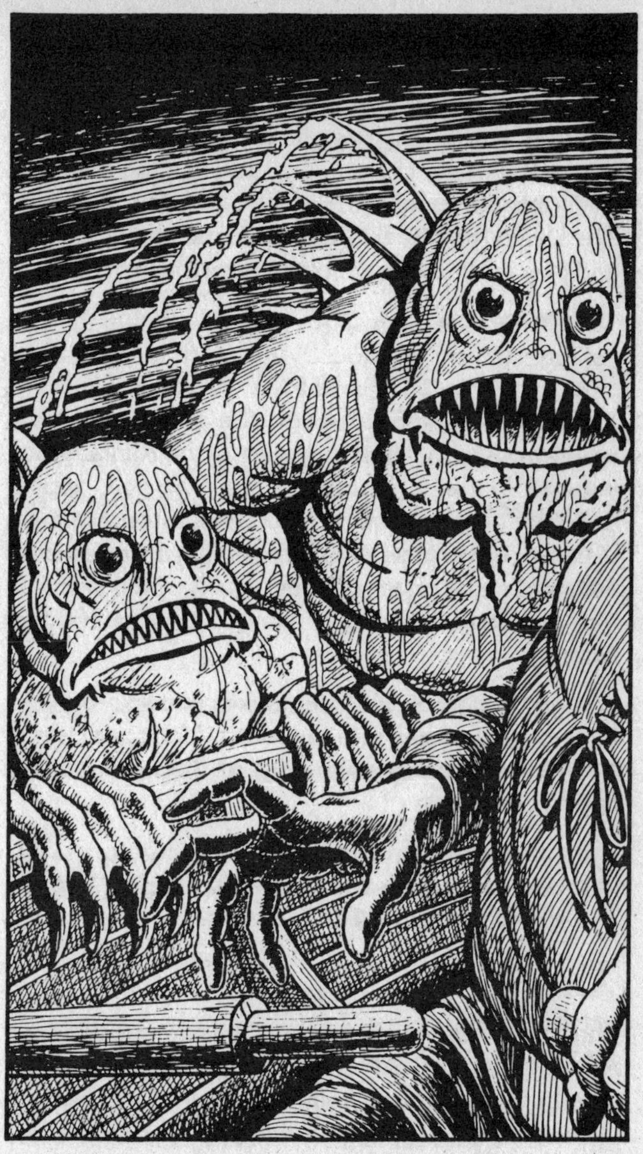

II. Suddenly ghoulish, dome-shaped heads rise from the river

30

The alarm bell signifies that the entrance to the tower is under attack. Adamas and his army have reached the centre of the city and are now fighting their way down into the dungeons in an attempt to free the slaves. The Death Knights are hurrying to their battle stations and they are unaware of your presence in this chamber.

Turn to **136**.

31

You rush headlong through the trees and dense undergrowth, the dreadful howls of the Akataz growing ever louder in your ears. The pine trees appear to be thinning out and, as you break through a mass of waist-high foliage, you discover that the forest ends abruptly at the edge of a steep gorge. You skid to a halt and stare down at a raging river over 100 feet below.

A snarl, dangerously close, makes you spin on your heel and stare back into the forest. Your gaze is met by a score of hungry war-dogs as they creep closer for the kill.

If you wish to stand and fight the Akataz, turn to **81**.
If you choose to evade them by jumping into the gorge, turn to **340**.

32

The Drakkarim give a loud yell as soon as they see Adamas appear. At once the vanguard fire their crossbows and many bolts find their mark, but the Drakkarim who fall do not hamper their comrades, who are preparing to welcome Adamas with huge chunks of rock. With cat-like agility he veers right and left, weaving his way through the deluge of falling boulders, which smash down with a terrific crack. He reaches the door unscathed, rips the satchel from his shoulder and primes the crystal explosive. Automatically you start to count as he runs back through rubble and dead bodies. Six . . . seven . . . eight . . . He leaps, and as you count nine he clears the rampart and lands beside you, breathless and exhilarated.

Turn to **301**.

33

Your lightning-fast reactions save you from the deadly blade. But even before the dagger has blunted itself on the wall behind, Halgar pulls free the Bullwhip that he carries on his belt. He lashes out and the copper-studded whip snakes towards your unprotected face.

Halgar: COMBAT SKILL 24 ENDURANCE 30

Owing to the speed of his attack you cannot use a bow or evade combat.

If you win the fight, turn to **145**.

34

You roll the dead Bhakish into the water and stare fearfully across the Hellswamp at myriad pairs of eyes gleaming coldly in the moonlight. A sudden movement in the water makes you recoil from the edge. Seconds later the scummy surface is whipped into a froth as the bodies are claimed by an unseen predator.

You and Jarel are unsettled by the encounter and you both spend a sleepless night cradling your weapons and waiting for the dawn: lose 2 ENDURANCE points.

Turn to **101**.

35

You stare deeply into the serpent's scarlet eyes and will the venomous creature to sleep. It begins to sway, then gradually its jaws close and it buries its head in its coils, succumbing totally to your command.

Turn to **205**.

36

With the legendary grace and speed of a Kai master in battle, you draw an arrow and send it whistling towards the sniper's head. He utters a gurgling scream as he topples from the first-floor window, your arrow stuck in his throat.

If you wish to run forward to search the body, turn to **296**.

If you choose to press on towards the centre of the town, turn to **155**.

37

You have covered less than a mile when suddenly you hear the screams of men and startled horses coming from the darkness ahead. Cautiously you advance until you find yourself at the edge of a steep slope which descends to the site of an ancient quarry. Torchlight flickers at the centre of this wooded bowl, illuminating a grim and supernatural conflict.

Turn to **266**.

38

Beyond the curtained arch lies a cavern bathed in the flickering light of a log fire. Five men sit cross-legged around the fire, carving meat from a boar on a spit suspended over the flames, and swilling wine from a wineskin that is passed between them.

'What have we here?' says a man with mouse-like features, as you appear before them.

'A Pathfinder, if I'm not mistaken,' says another, wiping spilt wine from his chin. 'Well, Pathfinder, what brings you to our camp?'

'I come to seek the help of Sebb Jarel,' you reply. 'Which one of you is he?'

'I am Jarel,' answers the mouse-like man. 'How can I aid you?'

If you have the Magnakai Discipline of Divination, turn to **157**.
If you do not possess this skill, turn to **275**.

39

You snatch the reins and wheel your horse around on its hind legs in one swift, elegant movement. The sergeant screams an order and his men lunge forward, hoping to stick you with their swords before your horse's forelegs return to the ground. But their attack is much too slow to catch a Kai master off-guard. Your horse regains its footing and you gallop through their shrinking ring of steel, barging aside two stout mountain ponies and leaving their riders sprawling in the dust.

The partisans give chase as you gallop headlong down a long and twisting hill track. You are beginning to out-distance your pursuers when your steed suddenly pitches forward and you are thrown head-first into a tangle of foliage. The dense undergrowth cushions your fall and you emerge unscathed, but your horse has been seriously injured. A deep pot-hole ensnared its foreleg and the limb is badly broken: the poor animal cannot go on. The partisans gallop into view and you are forced to abandon your crippled mount and escape on foot. With the angry cries of your pursuers growing ever louder, you curse your ill luck and run for the cover of the surrounding forest.

Turn to **250**.

40

The corroded iron gantry shakes violently as you inch your way nearer to the flaming green ball. Once you are in position, you call to Paido and, one by one, he smashes the crystal rods.

Turn to **196**.

41

Roark watches you rush towards him with hate and fear in his eyes. 'Help me, master,' he whimpers, rising unsteadily and drawing a slim-bladed sword from beneath his black robes.

Demonlord Tagazin answers his servant with a thunderous growl but does not hasten his pace to save him from your attack. He seems to be enjoying the fear that Roark displays, and as you strike his growl changes to a hideous snigger.

Roark: COMBAT SKILL 18 ENDURANCE 20

If you win and the fight lasts three rounds or less, turn to **326**.
If the fight lasts longer than three rounds, do not continue but turn instead to **10**.

42

'By the gods! What manner of black sorcery is this?' gasps Prince Graygor, horrified by the cruel slaughter. But his horror is soon overcome by the sudden realization that he must act swiftly to counter this threat or the battle might be lost. The Lencian knights are being held up at the bridge and every minute that passes costs them dearly.

He calls for his destrier, a magnificent white charger clad in ornate plate armour, and climbs into the saddle. 'To battle!' he shouts, and, ignoring the warnings of his heralds, he spurs his warhorse down the hill. The knights of the Palace Guard give a rousing cheer as he takes his place at the head of their column and leads them towards the ruined temple.

If you wish to mount your horse and join the cavalry advance, turn to **284**.

If you choose to stay where you are and observe the battle, turn to **163**.

43

With your heart in your mouth you leap across the raging river and land with a jolt that leaves you breathless. For several minutes you cling to the smooth rock until you are recovered enough to be able to continue to the far side. When you reach the safety of the opposite bank you discover that you have lost one item from your backpack – it must have fallen out as you made the jump.

Delete the item you have listed second on the Backpack section of your *Action Chart* before you venture into the Moggador Forest.

Turn to **186**.

44

You turn and race towards the bridge, but the way is now blocked by a barricade defended by Drakkarim archers. A clutch of black arrows screams through the air and you are forced to dive into an open doorway to avoid being hit. Swiftly you rise, crouched ready for combat lest an enemy is nearby waiting to attack you, but your caution proves unnecessary – the ruined cottage is empty.

After clambering through open windows and working your way across smouldering piles of rubble, you finally emerge at a street with a barn-like building on the corner. Crouching at a window on the upper floor is a Drakkar sniper with an arrow notched and ready to fire. He sees you appear and releases his straining bowstring, sending his arrow whistling towards your heart.

Pick a number from the *Random Number Table*. If you have the Magnakai Discipline of Huntmastery, add 3 to the number you have picked.

If your total is now *0–2*, turn to **264**.
If it is *3–5*, turn to **121**.
If it is *6* or more, turn to **319**.

45

Inside the tent a group of senior officers are poring over their battle-maps and planning their troop dispositions for an assault across the causeway. Their leader has his back to you, but when he turns to see who has entered his tent, you recognize him at once: he is Adamas, Lord Constable of Garthen. 'By the gods!' he exclaims. 'I thought the Danarg had claimed you, Lone Wolf. How good it is to see you alive.'

He dismisses his captains and bids you tell all that has happened since last you met. 'So you wish to break into Torgar,' he says, thoughtfully. 'How strange it is that our goals should be so similar. Come, follow me, perhaps co-operation will hasten our success.'

Turn to **127**.

46

Drawing on the combined power of your psychic skills, you focus a beam of clairvoyant energy at the captain's mind. Visions of warriors training with weapons and practising their woodcraft swirl before your eyes. You increase your concentration and suddenly a name crystallizes in your mind's eye.

'Sharwhan,' you say, confidently.

Turn to **287**.

47

You are about to descend when a shadow looms into view and a Drakkar officer appears at the foot of the stairs. Instantly you press yourself to the wall and use all your Kai skills to mask your presence. He strides up the stairs, passing within a few feet of you, but miraculously he fails to notice you and continues without stopping. After wiping the sweat from your brow you continue down the stairs.

Turn to **285**.

48

You tie one end of the rope to a strong stick and cast it across the gap. On your third attempt it anchors in some exposed tree roots near to the edge. A few tentative pulls assure you that it is secure enough to support your weight and you swing across, your feet braced to withstand the jolt of impact against the chasm wall.

Pick a number from the *Random Number Table*.

If the number you have picked is *0–4*, turn to **304**.
If it is *5–9*, turn to **289**.

49

Swiftly you inform the captains of the reserve regiments of the danger facing their Prince. At first they are reluctant to take orders from a Pathfinder, whose rank is inferior to theirs, but the logic of your argument and your forceful character persuades them to comply with your commands.

Trumpets announce the advance and you set off across the body-strewn battlefield with a force 900 strong. Pikemen lead the column with archers close behind, and bringing up the rear are a levy of militia, many of whom lived in Cetza before the Drakkarim invaded. Their morale is high for this is their chance to recover their homes and their land.

Tensely you watch as the enemy attack. The Palace Guard link shields but, as the Hammerlanders slam into their line, they buckle and waver beneath the crushing onslaught. As your force crosses the ditch, you pray that the Prince and his men have strength enough to hold for just a few minutes more.

Turn to **292**.

50

For several hours you follow an ancient pavement that mostly lies buried beneath the rich black soil of the forest floor. Occasionally you discover a heap of moss-covered slabs; they are all that remain of dwellings built long before the trees conquered the isle. It is late afternoon when you reach a clearing in the middle of which stands a decaying structure of mould-encrusted stone. The building is an immense ziggurat which is so overgrown that it appears to be a part of the surrounding soil and vegetation.

A section of this verdant growth has been cleared to reveal two massive doors of solid crystal set into the lowest level.

If you have the Magnakai Discipline of Divination, turn to **314**.

If you do not possess this skill, turn to **89**.

51 – *Illustration III*

A laugh, deep and guttural, rumbles from the far side of the cavern. 'I see Skalir's play-actin' ain't good enough to fool you, Pathfinder,' says a man who, until now, has been watching silently in the shadows. As he steps forward, the fire casts a warm glow over his massive frame. He stands over six-and-a-half-feet tall, his face is covered by a thick red beard and he has a shock of bright red hair that cascades over the wolfskin cloak slung over his shoulders. He smiles, his green eyes bright and piercing, set wide beneath an intelligent brow.

'Check on the sentries, Skalir,' he instructs his lieutenant. 'And make sure they've got their wits about 'em tonight.' Obediently, the mouse-like man and his four companions leave the chamber. As the curtain is pulled across the archway, the red-haired giant motions you to sit with him at the fire. 'I am Jarel,' he says. 'What do you want from me?'

Turn to **92**.

III. A massive man steps forward, with thick red hair and a beard that cascades over his wolfskin cloak

52

The plate-armoured warriors reach the bottom of the stairs and begin running in your direction, as fast as their heavy equipment will allow. Their ox-like leader urges them on with the words – 'Gaz darg! Gaz aga kuzim! Okim der tagog!'

If you have a bow and wish to use it, turn to **109**.
If you decide to draw a hand weapon and prepare for combat, turn to **320**.
If you choose to keep perfectly still in the hope that they have not seen you, turn to **136**.

53

'Excellent!' says King Sarnac. 'I wish I had a few like you in my own army.'

He bids you step forward and shows you the extent of the known enemy positions using Prince Graygor's map. Once you have been briefed, he sends for some black clothing for you to wear instead of your grey Pathfinder's uniform and some burnt cork with which to blacken your face and hands. You are then escorted to the edge of the encampment, close to the dusty road on which the army marched from Luomi. The guards tell you that the password is 'broadsword'. When you return you must use this word or the pickets – the sentries who guard the perimeter of the camp – may mistake you for one of the enemy.

Turn to **94**.

54

You land heavily at the edge of the chasm and the soil disintegrates on impact. Desperately you lunge for a tangle of roots and hold fast as your legs swing wildly in the void. Just as you begin to recover from the shock of the fall, you hear a scrabbling sound coming from somewhere deep within the rock face. Suddenly a section of the sheer wall crumbles away, exposing the head of a ghastly, worm-like creature with huge, clacking mandibles. You have disturbed a hungry Lapillibore and it is intent on eating you alive.

Lapillibore: COMBAT SKILL 16 ENDURANCE 50

Owing to your precarious position, deduct 3 points from your COMBAT SKILL for the duration of the fight. Unless you possess a weapon-like Special Item, reduce your COMBAT SKILL by a further 4 points and fight the creature unarmed.

If you win the combat, turn to **237**.

55

Slowly the ghosts encircle you and glide forward undaunted by the light. You brace yourself for their attack but still you shudder when their snaky tendrils lash out and engulf your limbs. Their touch fills you with a terrible chill that steals your strength and your will to resist. Reluctantly you surrender to their numbing caress and slip into a sleep from which there will be no awakening.

Your life and your quest end here.

56

The Ziran utters a gurgling, blood-soaked death cry, and crumples at your feet. Tongues of flame ignite and quickly consume his corpse beneath a pall of oily black smoke. Suddenly an explosion shakes the ground as the iron stave disintegrates into a million glowing shards. You rush to the injured Prince, heave him across your shoulder and flee the temple as the flames and choking black fumes begin to spread.

Once you are a safe distance from the ruins you lower the Prince gently to the ground and watch as the guttering flames gradually ebb and fade.

Turn to **211**.

57

The two robed figures utter a sinister curse and fling their globes into the air. The yellow spheres rise higher and higher until they disappear completely in the smoke-laden air. The Palmyrions are eager to engage the enemy and rush forward with their weapons drawn to strike. But before they fall upon the Drakkarim, the yellow spheres fall upon them – with devastating effect.

Turn to **106**.

58

The bear knows the forest well: he knows its treasures and its dangers. Carefully you follow in his tracks as he works his way through the pines towards the edge of a deep gorge, where a trail descends gently to the bank of a rushing river. Massive boulders, smoothed by centuries of erosion, rise from the foaming torrent like giant stepping stones. Across the river lies another forest, dark and forbidding. Although the sun is strong in the cloudless sky and the air is warm and dry, a grey mist hangs heavy and cold around the trees of that forest.

All along the bank on this side of the river grow clumps of bushy herbs with bright red flowers. The bear scoops a pawful of the scarlet petals and chews them contentedly as he nods farewell and ambles back into the forest.

If you have the Magnakai Discipline of Curing, turn to **276**.
If you do not possess this skill, turn to **325**.

59

The island is no more than a crusty mud flat supporting a brace of stunted trees. You make a landing and haul the boat out of the water before overturning it to provide a shelter from the monotonous drizzle. Your rumbling stomach reminds you that you have not eaten today, and you must eat a Meal now or lose 3 ENDURANCE points.

You agree to take the first watch and, as Jarel settles down to sleep, you sit and stare across the moonlit swamp, contemplating the journey ahead. By chance you are looking down at the water's edge when a scaly paw breaks through the surface and sinks its claws into the mud. A second paw joins it and between them rises a gruesome fish-like head. Moonlight glints on its needle-thin fangs as silently it slinks out of the mire.

If you have a bow and wish to use it, turn to **76**. If not, turn to **311**.

60

'You're a spy!' screams the captain as he reaches for the hilt of his sword. Instinctively you lash out, catching him with a powerful uppercut punch that lifts him clean off his feet and leaves him sprawled on the ground unconscious.

'Fire!' shouts a bull-necked Pirsian. You throw yourself to the floor. A deafening roar reverberates through the town as the men discharge their unwieldy pistols, but the lead shot passes harmlessly over your head and buries itself in the tavern door. The noise stirs a hornet's nest of activity as the rest of the townsfolk arm themselves and rush into the street to investigate the commotion. The situation is beginning to look desperate when you see a chance to escape. The pistols created a huge cloud of white smoke. Under cover of this acrid cloud you scurry along an alley beside the log tavern and run headlong into the foliage and trees beyond.

With the angry cries of the townsfolk rippling through the forest, you curse your ill luck as you make good your escape into the dark.

Turn to **250**.

61

The Talestrians bring their horses to a halt and regard you with suspicion. Their officer draws his sword and demands to know your nationality and the name of your regiment. You reply in his native tongue that you are an Eruan Pathfinder, and a smile spreads slowly across his rugged face. He tells you that he and his men are scouts who have been sent to make sure that the hills are free of enemy troops. Your Kai sixth sense confirms that he speaks the truth, and when he offers to take you to meet his commander, you accept the invitation gladly.

Turn to **6**.

62

The further you skirt around the edge of the chasm the wider it becomes. After an hour of searching for an alternative way across, you are forced to return to the trail and reconsider the jump.

If you have a rope and wish to use it, turn to **48**.
If not, turn to **317**.

63

The hail of arrows and the sight of your black-clad form lurching towards them makes the guards over-excited. They fear it is the beginning of a Drakkarim attack, and when they hear you shout the wrong password it makes them panic. 'Raid!' they cry, alerting a unit of crossbowmen stationed on the high ground behind them. They grab their loaded weapons and take aim, but the only target they can see is you.

A scything wave of iron bolts engulfs you and an agonizing explosion of pain fills your chest. You are mortally wounded and although you fight to hang on to your life, it is a struggle you cannot win.

Your life and your quest end here.

64

Blinding pain stabs at your head as pulses of psychic energy prise open the secrets of your mind: lose 5 ENDURANCE points. Lord Adamas commands you to reveal your mission and your true identity and you are powerless to resist.

Turn to **290**.

65

You recognize the emblem of Salony, the smallest of the Stornland nations. The two soldiers are dressed in the uniforms of mercenary swordsmen from the town of Amory, which is situated close to its northern border. Fear and suspicion grow stronger and you try to fathom a reason why these soldiers of fortune are here on this remote isle, 1000 miles from their homeland.

One of the men struggles to his feet and begins walking towards you. You sense that he has not seen you – he is merely answering the call of nature – but you decide that it is wise to slip away. Under cover of the forest you return to the front of the building.

Turn to **89**.

66

'On to Cetza!' shouts Prince Graygor. The battle-cry is taken up by his valiant soldiers as he leads them across the corpse-strewn field towards the town.

Heavy fighting is raging along the main street. The Lencian knights have taken the bridge and King Sarnac's spearmen have breached the wall that surrounds the apple orchard. However, the Drakkarim are determined to stand their ground and they fight back viciously like starving wolves. You run with a group of longbowmen towards the centre of Cetza and find yourself approaching a barn-like building which overlooks the bridge. Standing at a window on its upper floor is a Drakkar sniper with an arrow notched ready to fire. Patiently he watches you weaving through the smoky ruins until you present a clear target. He releases his straining bowstring and sends an arrow whistling towards your heart.

Pick a number from the *Random Number Table*. If you have the Magnakai Discipline of Huntmastery, add 3 to the number you have picked.

If your total is *0–2*, turn to **264**.
If it is *3–5*, turn to **121**.
If it is *6* or more, turn to **319**.

67

You have taken less than a dozen silent steps when the voices stop. There is a rustle of foliage, then a group of hideous-looking creatures emerge from the bushes. They are not as tall as you but almost twice as broad, with arms that hang below their knees. They slobber repulsively as they draw their primitive weapons and shuffle closer.

If you have a bow and wish to use it, turn to **119**. If not, turn to **315**.

68

With a yell, you barge your way through the stunned tavern crowd and kick open the back door. The land behind the building is thickly forested and you run headlong into its welcoming cover. With the angry cries of the Pirsians rippling through the trees, you curse your ill luck and escape into the darkness.

Turn to **250**.

69

'So you are Lone Wolf,' he says, bowing respectfully. 'I am honoured to meet you, though I would have wished for happier circumstances. I think I know why you have come to Torgar – is it not to take the golden gems which Darklord Gnaag sent here?'

'Yes,' you reply, 'they are the Lorestones of my ancestors and I have vowed to retrieve them. I must fulfil my vow for it is vital to the future safety of both our lands that Gnaag be prevented from destroying them.'

Slowly a smile spreads across Paido's face. 'I will help you, Lone Wolf,' he says, his warrior pride restored by the thought of avenging his cruel imprisonment. 'I know where these Lorestones are being held and I will take you there.'

Turn to **88**.

70

You draw an arrow and take aim at the creature's mouth. It howls with devilish glee, drawing back its lips in a snarl that reveals a jaw full of fangs, most over six inches long. As the smell of its fetid breath fills your nostrils, you release your arrow and send it streaking towards the beast's ghastly maw.

Pick a number from the *Random Number Table* and add any missile bonuses you may have.

If the total is now *0–2*, turn to **336**.
If it is *3–7*, turn to **349**.
If it is *8* or more, turn to **195**.

71

By the time you reach the ancient burial mound, Roark's follower is being drained of the last of his life-force by a host of hungry ghosts. Fear and premonition gnaw at your stomach when you sense that the evil spirits have detected your presence. They emit an unearthly shriek, and a terrible chill like a blast of icy cold wind washes over your body. You are gripped by an urge to run but they swoop down on you too quickly for you to be able to escape their clutches.

If you possess the Sommerswerd, turn to **133**.
If you possess a Bullwhip, turn to **168**.
If you possess neither of these Special Items, turn to **74**.

72

The creature emits a shrill whistle as your killing blow pierces its brain. Its deadly mandibles continue to snap spasmodically, but without purpose, as its lifeless body oozes from the hole and falls limply to the chasm floor.

Gripping firmly with both hands you haul yourself up, untie the stick from the end of the rope and wind it back into your pack before setting off deeper into the eerie forest.

Turn to **50**.

73

A shriek rises from the ranks of the Krorn as they catch the scent of your body drifting towards them on the breeze. Their heinous squeals alert Baron Shinzar to your presence and he turns to face you, his red axe glinting as a few rays of sunlight break through the haze of battle smoke.

If you possess the Sommerswerd, turn to **113**.
If you do not possess this Special Item, turn to **126**.

74

With your good hand you unsheathe your weapon and strike out at your ghostly attackers, but your brave blows pass clean through their mist-like forms without effect. You shudder with fear as their snaky tendrils close tightly around your limbs, filling them with a terrible chill that steals your strength and your will to resist. Reluctantly you surrender to their numbing caress and slip into a sleep from which there will be no awakening.

Your life and your quest end here.

75

The road beyond the river takes you into thick forest and a dense canopy of branches arches overhead. A dazzling mosaic of light and shade blankets the trail as it winds like a tunnel through the tall, grey-green trees. Gradually the trail becomes rougher: new saplings have speared through the stony surface and foliage spills out from the forest on either side. The tunnel ends abruptly at the edge of a steep valley, although the trail itself continues, winding its way down towards a fast-flowing stream.

76

Cautiously you urge your horse down the twisting path to arrive at a cluster of delapidated log huts. Rust and rot have taken their toll but you can still discern the remains of what was once a mining settlement where men panned for gold. A wooden sign hangs lop-sided above an open door, swinging slightly in the breeze. Its paint is cracked and the panel bears fresh sword scars, but you can still make out the words: it reads, KAIG SETTLEMENT.

Two trails lead away from this abandoned mining village. One climbs out of the valley and disappears into the forest; the other follows the stream towards its source among the snow-capped mountains of the Eru Range.

If you wish to take the trail that climbs out of the valley, turn to **313**.
If you wish to ride along the track beside the stream, turn to **18**.
If you have the Magnakai Discipline of Pathsmanship, turn to **102**.

76

You aim and fire in the blink of an eye, sending your arrow coursing deep into the creature's bloated body. It gives a sound more like a scream than a croak and sinks out of sight.

'What the. . . !?' coughs Jarel, woken by the scream. But before you can warn him, two more of the fish-like things clamber over the upturned boat and attack you both with their taloned paws.

Bhakish: COMBAT SKILL 21 ENDURANCE 25

These swamp dwellers are immune to Mindblast (but not Psi-surge).

If you win the combat, turn to **34**.

77 – *Illustration IV (overleaf)*

The gruesome clack of fangs fills your ears and white-hot pain lances through your arms and legs as the Akataz snap shut their powerful jaws. You try to repel them using your Kai mastery of Animal Control, but their blood fury is aroused and their minds are fixed unshakeably on rending you to shreds: lose 5 ENDURANCE points.

In desperation you will the black bear to come to your aid. It growls angrily and bounds towards the war-dogs. One snarling hound is wrenched from your leg, whirled about and flung into the forest to break its back against a tree. Another has its skull crushed between the bear's powerful paws, and a third is torn to ribbons by one swipe of its razor-sharp claws. With your arms now free you are able to draw a weapon and dispatch an Akataz that has its fangs caught in the sole of your boot. Freed at last from your attackers, you sit up in time to see the bloodied survivors slinking away into the undergrowth.

Turn to **117**.

78

'It's an impressive-looking door,' says Adamas, studying the wall of black iron, pitted and streaked with age. 'But every door has its key, and we have the key to this one.' He flips open the leather satchel and removes

IV. The black bear wrenches one snarling hound from your leg and another is torn to shreds by its razor-sharp claws

what appears to be a mass of triangular crystals fused into one solid lump. 'This is the device that the Elder Magi prepared for us. It has to be placed at the foot of the door and it is activated by pressing this shard,' he says, pointing to a sliver of crystal protruding from the side. 'The thing explodes ten seconds after the shard is pressed.'

Calmly he takes a coin from his pocket and flicks it in the air. 'One of us must place the device,' he says, as he catches the coin. 'We're the only two left who stand a chance of surviving the run.' He nods at his clenched fist and invites you to call 'heads' or 'tails'.

If you wish to call 'heads', turn to **330**.
If you wish to call 'tails', turn to **212**.
If you have the Magnakai Discipline of Divination and wish to use it, turn to **14**.

79

Once you have managed to grab hold of his arms you heave him out from beneath his dead mount and prise open the visor of his helmet. He coughs and retches the mud from his mouth and lies back against the bank of the ditch.

'I owe you my life, Pathfinder,' he gasps. 'Another minute and I'd have been done for.' You turn to leave but he grabs you by the wrist and presses a Medal into your hand. 'I won this at the Battle of Luomi,' he says with pride. 'I want you to have it, with my eternal thanks.' (If you wish to keep the Medal, mark it on your *Action Chart* as a Special Item that you carry in your pocket.)

80

Another cloud of arrows falls from the sky and you dive to the bottom of the ditch to avoid being hit. When you feel it is safe to raise your head, you discover that the knight is no longer with you: he is chasing after the Prince and his fellow knights as they gallop up the hill towards the Drakkarim pikemen.

If you wish to follow him on foot, turn to **115**.
If you decide to look for a horse, turn to **247**.

80

The lock clicks and the door opens on to a passage lined with torches that splutter and crackle noisily. Halfway along there is another door – a solid slab of iron broken only by a small, barred window. Silently you approach this door and peer in through the grille.

If you have visited the Danarg in a previous Lone Wolf adventure, turn to **260**.
If not, turn to **114**.

81

The Akataz fling themselves at you with wild ferocity, as if they are hungry to avenge the deaths of their brothers.

Akataz Pack: COMBAT SKILL 28 ENDURANCE 45

These war-dogs are especially susceptible to psychic attack. If you possess the Discipline of Mindblast or Psi-surge and wish to use either of them, double all bonuses you would normally receive. If you have completed the Lore-circle of the Spirit, triple all bonuses.

You can evade combat at any time by leaping into the gorge: turn to **340**.
If you win the combat, turn to **268**.

82

Upon hearing your reply the officer lowers his sword and a friendly smile spreads across his rugged face. He tells you that he and his men are Talestrian scouts who have been sent ahead of their army to make sure these hills are free of enemy troops. Your Kai sixth sense confirms that he is speaking the truth, and when he offers to take you to meet his commander, you accept the invitation gladly.

Turn to **6**.

83

Your Kai skill enables your body to overcome the intoxicating effect of the scent. Shaking your head and stiffling a yawn, you urge your horse towards the end of the gorge.

Turn to **98**.

84

You search the bodies of the dead Krorn but find little of value. Their weapons are crude and poorly fashioned, and their packs contain nothing but strips of dried meat. You consider the long journey ahead, but stories you have heard about the Krorn's love of human flesh are enough to put you off the idea of taking this food.

If you wish to hide the bodies before you cross the river, turn to **146**.
If you choose to leave them where they lie, turn to **335**.

85

Sebb Jarel informs the partisans that he has agreed to guide you through the Hellswamp. He is careful not to reveal details of your quest, but he does tell them that your mission has royal approval and, if successful, will strike a major blow against the Drakkarim and their Darklord masters.

At dawn, after a good night's sleep and a hearty breakfast, you mount and ride along a hidden trail that leads to Pirsi. There you leave your horses, for the next part of your journey, through Forest Taintor, is too difficult to attempt on horseback. Following traces of a forgotten path, you trek through the blue-grey pines until twilight when you stop to make camp for the night. Jarel volunteers for the first watch while you settle down gratefully on a bed of leaf mould and drift off into a dreamless sleep.

It feels as if you have only just closed your eyes when you are awoken by the savage and desolate howl of a Taintor wolf.

Turn to **329**.

86

Your senses tell you that this man is both trustworthy and highly intelligent. There would be little to gain from trying to deceive him. It occurs to you that with his help it would be far easier for you to gain entry to Torgar and attempt the retrieval of the Lorestones. After careful consideration you decide to reveal your identity.

Turn to **290**.

87

Four men die before the shield wall knits together and the lost ground is regained. The Hammerlanders reel back and the Brigandi surge forward, but they too cannot break through the Palace Guard. A trumpet sounds in the distance and the Prince's men cheer when they see their reserves streaming up the hill to support them. Two hundred Eruan pikemen press forward behind their bristling steel and take the enemy in the flank. The attack is devastating. The enemy are split asunder and swept from the slope. The pikemen halt and through their ranks a wave of archers moves forward to fire at the backs of the retreating foe. Retreat turns to rout as the Hammerlanders and Brigandi flee the field in chaos.

Turn to **66**.

88 – *Illustration V*

Stealthily you follow Paido through the dungeons of Torgar, using the shadows to avoid being seen. Ragged columns of slaves stumble along the passages, dragging their tortured, half-starved bodies to and from the work pits. They are beaten, cursed and whipped relentlessly by their Drakkarim guards, who seem to delight in their suffering.

You emerge from a corridor into the shadows of a circular chamber, where a staircase ascends to a pair of huge triangular iron doors guarded by a squad of crack Drakkarim Death Knights. A tingling sensation electrifies your skin as your senses detect the presence of the Lorestones somewhere behind these doors. Suddenly an alarm bell fills the chamber with a deafening clangour; the Death Knights begin to descend the stairs and your stomach churns with the fear that you have been detected.

If you have the Magnakai Discipline of Divination, turn to **299**.

If you do not possess this skill, turn to **52**.

89

Curiosity overcomes your natural caution and you decide to investigate the fascinating structure. You discover that the undergrowth has only recently been chopped away to give access to the doors where gaping, fire-blackened holes are all that remain of the crystal locks that held them secure for centuries. Beyond the damaged doors a dry, dark tunnel slopes gently downwards. It twists as it descends to a chamber, which is huge and empty, and ringed by a

V. Ragged columns of slaves stumble along the passages, beaten, cursed and whipped by their Drakkarim guards

score of openings. A green glow and the faint thrumming of discordant chanting draws you to one of these many portals. Beyond it a staircase delves deeper into the earth.

As you make your way carefully downward, the air becomes increasingly humid and chill. The stairs are slick with moisture and crawling with spiders and other many-legged creatures that scuttle away from your feet. You count sixty steps before the staircase ends at a huge door stained black with damp and age. It is slightly ajar and, as you peer through the crack, you are chilled to the core by what lies beyond.

Turn to **200**.

90

You share an evening meal with a company of longbowmen camped close to the Prince's tent. Most of them are tired after the long day's march and when the meal is over they settle down to sleep. However, there are several who cannot sleep and, in order to take their minds off the coming battle, they busy themselves either by notching their arrows and waxing their bowstrings, or by gambling with dice. Two archers from Humbold invite you to join in their game.

If you wish to join their game of dice, turn to **218**.
If you choose instead to return to the Prince's tent, turn to **29**.

91

White-hot pain explodes through your chest and neck as three black-shafted Drakkarim arrows sink deep into your body. You scream in agony as you fall to the ground, but the pain quickly gives way to a terrifying numbness that robs you of all resistance to death.

Your life and your quest end here.

92

The partisan leader listens patiently as you recount the many events that led you to seek his help. He sits staring into the fire, his eyes fixed on the flickering flames as he digests every word you say and considers their consequences carefully. At length, having heard your earnest appeal for him to guide you, he raises his eyes from the fire and holds you with their piercing gaze.

'You speak with courage and wisdom, Kai lord. It is rare to find these virtues present so strongly in one so young. The help you beg me to provide could cost my life, yet you offer no reward, save the thanks of some distant land and the slender promise of a better age. However, I feel compelled to help you, for in my heart I know you are the one who can deliver us from the perpetual shadow of the Darklords.'

He rises and bids you follow him as he walks to the archway. 'Come, we must prepare for our journey. The road you wish to travel is perilous and long. We had best set off at the earliest, lest caution and common sense change my mind.'

Turn to **85**.

93

Your psychic defences alert you to deadly danger. The swirling shapes that you see are the ghosts of Cener druids who were slain on the isle many centuries ago.

They have been drawn from their forgotten graves by the presence of their master, Tagazin, and now they come to enact the Demonlord's revenge by feasting on your life-force.

The creatures take to the air and emit a ghastly howl as they draw closer. They sense your strong psychic defences and know instinctively that to steal your life-force will not be an easy task.

If you possess the Sommerswerd, turn to **133**.
If you do not possess this Special Item, turn to **256**.

94

The ground to the west of Cetza is flat and featureless and offers very little cover to conceal your approach. Slowly you work your way through the knee-high grasses to within twenty yards of a stone bridge, where the roadway crosses a foul-smelling ditch and enters the town. Your every movement is stiff with caution now, for the bridge is barracaded and you can see the spiky black helmets of the enemy defenders glinting in the moonlight. Snake-like you wriggle forwards, slide down into the ditch and take shelter beneath the stone

bridge. With one cheek pressed against the wet stone you strain your ears to hear what the enemy are saying. You recognize their harsh, ugly language – it is Giak – but it is being spoken by human voices. The only humans to speak it so fluently are the Death Knights, the elite of the Drakkarim.

Suddenly there is a loud splash that sends your pulse racing: a spear has fallen close to where you are hiding and its shaft stands upright in the muddy water. A growling curse is followed by the sound of heavy boots descending the bank as an angry Death Knight comes to retrieve the weapon he dropped.

If you have completed the Lore-circle of Solaris, turn to **13**.

If you do not possess mastery of this Lore-circle, pick a number from the *Random Number Table*. If you possess the Magnakai Discipline of Invisibility, add 2 to the number you have picked.

If your total is now *0–6*, turn to **107**.
If it is 7 or more, turn to **338**.

95

You smite the chain a mighty blow but you miss the rivet and the link does not break. Incensed by the boldness of your attack, and aware now of the threat it would have posed had it succeeded, the Demonlord leaps upon you and sinks his fangs deep into your chest. Pain explodes in your body but the agony is soon obliterated by the numbing chill of death.

Your life and your quest end here.

96

The Baron is shouting at the Krorn to form a line and get ready to advance. The only vulnerable part of his body that you can see as he strides back and forth before his troops is his unarmoured head.

Coolly you draw an arrow to your lips and aim at the nape of his neck.

Pick a number from the *Random Number Table* and add to it any bonuses you may have.

If your total is now *0–7*, turn to **9**.
If your total is now *8* or more, turn to **272**.

97

For an hour you sit staring at the river, mourning the loss of your brave companion. Your heart is heavy with the grief of his passing but you do not permit sorrow to become despair. You turn your eyes towards Torgar and defiantly you vow to avenge his death by retrieving the stolen Lorestones from the dungeons of that dread citadel.

Your journey along the bank of the River Torg is a long and tiring ordeal. For eight days you trudge through the black mud, cut off from all view of the lands to the north and south by an unbroken wall of stunted trees. The only inhabitants of this forsaken territory are the buzzing insects which hang seemingly motionless in the humid air. They are a constant source of irritation but at least their bite proves harmless.

On the morning of the ninth day, the muddy river bank gives way to firmer ground and the trees become less dense. Ahead you can see a barren expanse of yellow sulphurous soil that marks the beginning of the Nadulrit-zaga foothills. You can also see a road of broken stones disappearing into the distance.

Turn to **140**.

98

A sudden tumble of loose shale from the rim of the gorge alerts you to potential danger. You focus your eagle eyes on the rugged grey rocks above and catch sight of a pair of eyes staring down at you through a gap between two large boulders. Your stomach tightens. You feel trapped, and are about to spur your horse towards the mouth of the gorge and escape, when a voice calls down from above: 'Hail Pathfinder! What news have you from Luomi?'

If you choose to answer the voice, turn to **223**.
If you decide to make a hasty escape from the gorge, turn to **134**.

99

The shouts of the defenders and the metallic twang

of the vanguard's crossbows echo across the causeway as you sprint headlong towards the door. A rain of boulders begins to fall, smashing around you with terrific force, but you manage to dodge these and reach your goal unscathed. Quickly you tear the satchel from your shoulder, prime the crystal explosive, and sprint back, counting the seconds with every step. Suddenly a terrific jolt throws you forward and a dull throbbing pain spreads across your back. A falling rock has clipped your shoulder blade and knocked you to the ground: lose 4 ENDURANCE points.

Desperation suppresses the pain and you scramble over the rampart with only one second to spare.

Turn to **301**.

100

Cautiously you approach the edge of the pit and look down into its midnight depths. No light penetrates the blackness and no sounds can be heard in this seemingly bottomless abyss.

Above you the Lorestones hang suspended in a ball of green flame, beyond reach from the ground but within a hand's breadth of the gantries which criss-cross above the pit.

If you wish to climb a gantry and attempt to retrieve the Lorestones from above, turn to **249**.
If you wish to examine the crystal rods, turn to **160**.
If you wish to search for a way of retrieving the Lorestones from below, turn to **201**.

101

The third day of your voyage is accompanied by a cold west wind that blows across the desolate swamp and chills you to the bone. Clumps of twisted grey foliage line the channel along which you row, releasing nauseating clouds of gas as your bow-wave laps at their rotting roots. At length, you pass by these poisoned shrubs and reach a wider water-way where the current flows against you.

'We must be getting near the Torg estuary,' says Jarel, now having to labour at the oars in order to make head-way. He continues for a few minutes more, then, just as you are about to take your turn at rowing, the mouth of the River Torg looms into view.

Turn to **209**.

102

Your Kai sense tells you that the trail that climbs out of the valley is heading north. The town of Pirsi lies approximately thirty miles in that direction.

If you wish to take this trail and head north to Pirsi, turn to **313**.

(continued over)

If you choose to follow the track upstream towards the west, turn to **18**.

103

Having made sure that your pack and other equipment are securely fastened, you take a long run-up and leap feet-first across the gap.

Pick a number from the *Random Number Table*. If you have the Magnakai Discipline of Huntmastery add 3 to the number you have picked.

If your total in now *0–6*, turn to **154**.
If it is 7 or more, turn to **215**.

104

You recognize the pale, badly scarred features of Roark, lord of the Salonese town of Amory. He has aged much since your last meeting: his jet black hair is now streaked with grey and he walks with a stoop, as if burdened by a heavy pack. But his eyes are still as cold and as cruel as they were when he attempted to kill you four years ago.

Turn to **263**.

105

'I come from King Sarnac,' says the officer, his voice full of urgency. 'I must find your Prince and request that he commit his reserves at once in support of our knights assaulting the bridge. Our spearmen are already engaged in a desperate attack at the orchard and the rest of our retainers have been used to support our cavalry advance on the right flank. We have but less than 100 men left to save our noblemen, who are being slaughtered at the bridge.'

You tell the officer where the Prince and his Palace Guard are fighting, of their victory, and of the desperate situation they now face. 'I understand,' says the officer, sadly. 'I cannot expect the Prince to allow his reserves to be used when he needs them so urgently himself.'

If you wish to return and take command of the Prince's reserves, turn to **49**.
If you wish to help the Lencian officer gather reinforcements to support the knights at the bridge, turn to **148**.

106

You are dazzled by a brilliant flash as the two globes explode, scattering fragments that hiss like a host of fiery snakes into the Palmyrion ranks. The men-at-arms scream with pain and terror as the fragments burn everything they touch. You cannot escape the worst of the blast, but the sleeve of your tunic is splashed with fragments and is now on fire.

If you have the Magnakai Discipline of Nexus and have reached the Kai rank of Principalin or more, turn to **2**.
If you do not possess this skill, or have yet to reach this level of Kai training, turn to **253**.

107

With a splash, the Death Knight warrior appears, his massive frame filling the archway. He curses his clumsiness and snatches up his spear, but his curses turn to shouts of alarm when he sees you hiding beneath the bridge.

If you wish to attack this elite Drakkar soldier, turn to **180**.

(continued over)

If you wish to escape from beneath the bridge and run for the safety of the allies' camp, turn to **316**.
If you have the Magnakai Discipline of Psi-surge and wish to use it, turn to **139**.

108

You ride along an overgrown cart track that descends to the ford. As you draw level with the first log hut, your horse rears up and whinnies as if sensing danger, and you are forced to tighten your grip of the reins for fear of being thrown. As you regain control of your mount there is a sudden shout and a hail of arrows comes whistling towards you.

Pick a number from the *Random Number Table*. If you have the Magnakai Discipline of Huntmastery and Animal Control, add 3 to the number you have picked.

If your total is now *0–1*, turn to **91**.
If it is *2–6*, turn to **283**.
If it is *7* or more, turn to **153**.

109

At point-blank range your arrow strikes the Drakkar leader's armour with lethal force; it punches through the thick metal plate which protects his chest and skewers his heart. As he crashes to the ground, the other warriors draw their swords and rush forward to avenge his death.

Elite Death Knights:
COMBAT SKILL 38 ENDURANCE 45

If you win the combat, turn to **162**.

110

King Sarnac and a host of mounted knights block the road that leads to Blackshroud. They sit astride their warhorses, their armour dented and stained with the blood of the Baron's cavalry, all of whom they have slain in battle or put to flight. The Baron thunders towards them at breakneck speed, but the King and his knights remain grimly immobile, like a wall of tarnished steel. Slowly they lower their lances as the Baron speeds nearer and nearer. With a last defiant cry of anger, the Baron and his horse smash headlong into the line. There is a sickening screech of buckling metal and rearing horses, then the Baron reappears, hoisted into the air, impaled on the tip of King Sarnac's lance.

Turn to **300**.

111

The captain smiles. Then he looks over your shoulder and nods to the owner. You hear a thin squeak followed by a rush of air as the crossbow bolt hurtles towards your back. Your Kai senses scream a warning and you respond by flattening yourself to the table. A look of abject terror barely has time to register on the captain's face before the speeding missile embeds itself between his startled eyes.

'Get him!' screams the owner, and three stocky drinkers rush forward with short swords held ready to strike. The first attacker loses his sword and the hand that holds it. As he reels back, screaming, the others exchange a fearful glance and halt in their tracks.

If you wish to advance and attack them, turn to **274**.
If you decide to try to escape from the log tavern, turn to **68**.

112

You focus your Kai skill on the lumbering reptile and command it to retreat. It halts and raises its horned head, its hungry eyes regarding you with suspicion. Then, with a snort of disdain, it turns and crawls back into the tall grass.

Turn to **144**.

113 – *Illustration VI*

'Meet your doom, Eruan scum!' he sneers, as he strides across the square, his fearsome axe raised to strike. You lift the Sommerswerd and level it at his head; the blade shimmers gold as the sunlight catches upon its tip and charges it with power. A flicker of doubt passes across the Baron's eyes, but he shrugs aside his fear and continues to advance. With a roar like a howling gale the blade of his axe is transformed into a mass of scarlet flame that reeks of sulphurous decay.

Baron Shinzar (with Ogg-kor-kaggaz):
COMBAT SKILL 40 ENDURANCE 50

Intoxicated by the power of the weapon he wields, the Baron is immune to Mindblast (but not Psi-surge).

You may evade combat after three rounds; turn to **229**.

If you win the combat, turn to **300**.

114

You see a dank dungeon cell and a prisoner sitting crosslegged on the cold stone floor. His dark skin is covered with tiny scars and his plaited flaxen hair is matted with grime and dried blood. Wearily he raises his head and his sharp cat-like eyes glint in the torch-

VI. 'Meet your doom, Eruan scum!' he sneers, his fearsome axe raised to strike

light. At once you recognize his distinctive features: he is a Vakeros, a native warrior-magician of Dessi.

You step back to examine the lock and notice that the key to this cell is hanging on a hook beside the door.

If you wish to open the cell and release the prisoner, turn to **269**.

If you decide to ignore him and continue, turn to **189**.

115

Prince Graygor's voice rings out above the din of battle as he orders the Palace Guard to charge the pikemen. The ground shakes beneath the pounding of the horse's hooves as they gather speed, their pennons streaming from their levelled lances. The Drakkarim huddle shoulder to shoulder and nervously dig the butts of their pikes into the hillside to steady their shaky hands. The knights reach the hill. They thunder up the slope. A blaze of lightning hurtles from the top of the temple but it is mistimed: it crackles harmlessly over their heads and explodes behind them, hurling nothing but scorched earth into the sky. The Prince screams his battle-cry and the knights slam into the Drakkarim with a deafening roar. Men and metal howl in agony as the heavy horses break like a wave against the wall of pikes. You see a rider lifted out of his saddle on the point of a pike, and a ramp of black metal suddenly appears where a score of Drakkarim have been trampled into the ground. The Prince and a dozen of his bravest knights break through and gallop on towards the temple, but the Drakkarim quickly close ranks and seal the gap. The remaining Palace Guard are forced to a halt and engage the pikemen in fierce hand-to-hand combat.

You reach the hill and leap over the steel-clad bodies that litter the slope. As you near the mêlée you see two Drakkarim rushing towards you from the side, their axes raised to hack you down. 'For Sommerlund!' you cry, and turn to face their attack.

Drakkarim: COMBAT SKILL 22 ENDURANCE 32

If you win the combat, turn to **297**.

116 – *Illustration VII (overleaf)*

The swirling mists draw in towards the marble block. They grow darker as they merge into a solid shape that resembles a huge, sabre-toothed jackal with smooth creamy-coloured skin. Ice sheens on his muscular body and wisps of black smoke curl from his snuffling snout. Roark and his followers throw themselves to their knees and praise the creature devoutly. He responds by lowering his glowing eyes and regarding them with disdain.

'Why do you summon me here?' he says, his voice deep and rasping. But before Roark can offer a reply, the Demonlord swivels his head in your direction and emits a fearful snarl.

If you have the Magnakai Discipline of Psi-screen, turn to **26**.
If you do not possess this skill, turn to **213**.

117

The bear looks down at you kindly and raises its blood-stained paw. Gently it hooks a razor-sharp claw under

VII. A huge, sabre-toothed jackal with smooth creamy-coloured skin regards them with disdain

the strap of your backpack and lifts you to your feet. Having just witnessed the power and ferocity of the creature, you are amazed at how tame it has become under the influence of your Kai mastery. Suddenly something in the air disturbs him and you sense that he wants to leave this place, and he wants you to follow.

If you wish to follow the bear, turn to **58**.
If not, turn to **3**.

118

The sergeant screams an order and his men lunge forward, hoping to skewer you with their long straight swords. Coolly you parry their first attack and retreat just far enough to prevent them from getting behind you. With a yell of anger and frustration, the sergeant urges his men to attack you once more.

Partisan Horsemen:
COMBAT SKILL 28   ENDURANCE 32

If you have the Magnakai Discipline of Animal Control, add 2 points to your COMBAT SKILL for the duration of the fight.

You can evade combat after two rounds of fighting; turn to **39**.
If you win the combat, turn to **239**.

119

You draw an arrow and let it fly at the leading creature. It pierces its hairless skull and sends it reeling into the bushes. The others gurgle their displeasure and fix you with their murderous black eyes as they make ready to rush forward and attack.

Krorn: COMBAT SKILL 20   ENDURANCE 33

If you win the combat, turn to **84**.

120

The hoarse cries of soldiers and the blare of war trumpets announce preparations for an assault across the causeway. Armoured infantry gather in a spearhead formation and wait for the order to advance towards a wall of logs and earth, which has been thrown up to protect the vanguard troops dug in on the causeway itself. These warriors scuttle about behind their ramparts, holding arched wooden shields over their bent backs to protect them against the arrows raining down from the battlements. The iron gate stands less than fifty yards from their position, and this approach is heaped with the bodies of those who have fallen during previous assaults.

You accompany Lord Adamas as he makes his way through the massed ranks of infantry and enters a trench which zig-zags towards the causeway. He stops at a log-lined hollow dug out of the trench wall and speaks with a captain who is lying there nursing a broken arm. The wounded officer hands him his leather satchel, and Adamas continues along the trench until he reaches the centre of the causeway. There you both take cover with the vanguard and peer through a slit in the log wall at the formidable entrance to Torgar.

Turn to **78**.

121

Instinct saves you from sudden death. You twist aside to avoid the speeding shaft and it grazes your shoulder:

lose 2 ENDURANCE points. But your enemy is now determined that you should die and hastily he reloads his bow.

If you have a bow and wish to use it, turn to **36**.
If you wish to dive for cover among the ruins, turn to **277**.
If you wish to evade the sniper by running along an alley to your left, turn to **155**.

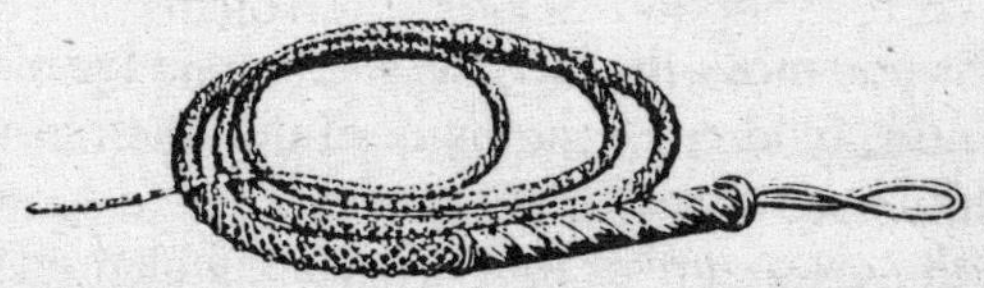

122

When the horsemen catch sight of you they unsheathe their swords and bring their steeds to a halt. Their leader dismounts and approaches you with trepidation, his gleaming steel blade held ready in case of trickery. With nervous eyes he studies your travel-stained tunic while his men scour the surrounding hills.

'What's your regiment, soldier?' he demands gruffly. You return his strong stare and notice that he and his men are wearing red and grey surcoats embroidered with the emblem of an open hand. The only horsemen who wear this livery are the cavalry of Talestria.

If you wish to tell the officer that you are an Eruan Pathfinder, turn to **82**.
If you decide to tell him that you are a Sommlending Kai Lord, turn to **339**.
If you choose not to answer him at all, turn to **151**.

123

The jump is made more hazardous by a tangle of trees and roots that cover the far side of the chasm. However, these obstacles do offer a secure anchor for a rope.

If you have a rope and wish to use it, turn to **48**. If not, turn to **317**.

124

Silently you move through the shallow sludge of water and mud, hidden by the bank of the ditch from the watchful eyes of the Drakkarim sentries. Beyond the ditch the ground rises to a low wall, which encircles a field of cultivated trees. It is an apple orchard and it is full of enemy soldiers, huddled around their campfires or asleep beneath the fruit-laden branches. Beyond the orchard lies an expanse of open grassland covered with tents and makeshift paddocks full of horses. Here then are Baron Shinzar's reinforcements – over 600 cavalry newly arrived from Blackshroud. You commit every detail to memory before leaving the ditch and making your way back stealthily to the allies' camp.

The King and Prince Graygor praise the success of your scouting mission: the information you have gathered is of vital importance to their battle plans. The Prince senses that you are tired and orders his heralds to escort you back to his headquarters and prepare a comfortable bed for you. After the long day's march and the exertions of your scouting mission, you accept gratefully the chance of a good night's sleep.

Turn to **280**.

125

Your journey northwards thr ugh the Moggador Forest is a long and tiring trek that is fraught with danger. Roving bands of Krorn and packs of savage timber wolves demand that you remain vigilant at all times, and as you venture deeper into their vast domain, you feel your sense of time gradually slipping away. Your only consolation on this long and lonely trek is that wild game is plentiful and you experience no shortage of food.

On the morning of your ninth day in the forest you notice that the grey pines are beginning to thin out and the ground is becoming dusty and sparsely vegetated. Soon you come upon a road constructed of broken stones which leaves the forest and disappears into a barren landscape of yellow sulphurous soil. You check your map and it confirms your suspicions: you have reached the foothills of the Nadulritzaga Mountains and are now less that twenty miles from the fortress of Torgar.

Turn to **140**.

126 – *Illustration VIII (overleaf)*

Baron Shinzar snarls an order and the Krorn pack move towards you. They are not as tall as their leader but almost twice as broad, with arms like branches of a twisted tree that hang down below their knees. Awkwardly they shuffle on short bow legs, their gnarled skin shiny like knotted leather. A shiver runs down your spine as you recall what you have heard about these creatures – that they delight in eating their foes – but as they draw nearer you dismiss such thoughts and prepare for combat.

VIII. The Krorn pack shuffle towards you on short bow legs, their gnarled skin shiny like knotted leather

Krorn Pack: COMBAT SKILL 23 ENDURANCE 60

If you win the combat and the fight lasts four rounds or less, turn to **11**.

If the fight lasts longer than four rounds, turn to **321**.

127

A short distance from Lord Adamas's tent stands a wooden watchtower, constructed by his army engineers, which offers an unobstructed view of the causeway and the great gate of Torgar. As you reach the top of its rickety ladder and step on to the platform beside the Lord Constable, he recounts the events that have led to the siege of this city-fortress.

Following his victory over the Ogians and the destruction of Xanar, Adamas led the allied armies of Bor, Talestria and Palmyrion along the Blackshroud Trail in pursuit of the shattered enemy. When they reached the Agna-kor-kuzim, the 'road of slaves', the army of Bor was detached and sent to assail Blackshroud from the east, while the bulk of the allied forces marched north towards Torgar. When Talestria was overrun in the early days of the war, thousands of her people were taken as slaves and imprisoned here in this fortress. Lord Adamas had sworn that one day he would free them and he was determined to fulfil his pledge.

During the march north a great battle was fought near the wastelands of Zuttezna, against two Giak armies led by Darklord Kraagenskul and Darklord Chlanzor. Both were soundly defeated by the allies and sent back to Cragmantle to lick their wounds. Although victorious at Zuttezna, the allies had suffered heavy losses and

Adamas feared they would be too weak to storm Torgar. He was too far from his homeland for reinforcements to reach him swiftly, and there was the growing threat that the Darklords would muster their troops in Tanoz and Mozgôar and attack again. Faced with this grave dilemma he decided to risk an assault on Torgar.

'We have means to breach their iron gate,' he says, staring purposefully at the great door of Torgar. 'The Elder Magi have given us a device that will reduce it to twisted scrap, and when we march through that portal and free our people, we shall have all the reinforcements we need.'

Turn to **120**.

128

The clasp that secures the amulet to the black chain around Tagazin's neck is a riveted link of iron. To break this link you must strike a blow that will destroy the rivet.

Pick a number from the *Random Number Table*. If the weapon you are using is a dagger or a quarterstaff, deduct 3 from the number you have picked. If the weapon you are using is an axe or a mace, add 1 to the number. If you possess the Magnakai Discipline of Huntmastery, add 2 to the number.

If your total is now 6 or less, turn to **95**.
If it is 7 or more, turn to **233**.

129

You push open the tower door with your foot and a splash of morning sunlight illuminates the gloomy interior. Slowly the man raises his weather-browned face and a smile softens his craggy features as he recognizes the uniform you are wearing.

'Welcome, Pathfinder,' he says, his thick Eruan accent echoing around the empty stone chamber. 'I am Halgar of Pirsi. Come and share my humble feast in celebration of our victory over the Drakkarim.'

He splits the roasted bird in two and tosses half to you. It tastes delicious. 'I saw you approaching,' he says, wiping away the grease from his mouth with the back of a calloused hand, 'and I wagered you would stop to breakfast here. Where are you bound?'

You hesitate to answer, but your basic Kai sixth sense tells you that this man is no trickster. 'I'm riding to Pirsi. I've orders to contact Sebb Jarel,' you reply, hoping he will offer to tell you where the partisan leader may be found. Halgar narrows his sea-green eyes and strokes his chin thoughtfully.

If you have the Magnakai Discipline of Invisibility, turn to **331**.
If you do not possess this skill, turn to **267**.

130

You examine the lock and recognize its simple latch mechanism.

If you possess the Magnakai Discipline of Nexus, turn to **328**.
If you possess a dagger, turn to **142**.
If you possess neither this skill nor this weapon, turn to **17**.

131

You draw an arrow and take aim at an archer just as he raises his bow to fire at you. Your shaft beats his: it buries itself in his chest and sends him spinning to the ground. Quickly you note that of the five men advancing towards you two are armed with bows.

If you have at least two arrows in your quiver and wish to fire at these men, turn to **344**.
If you wish to try to escape by crossing the ford, turn to **166**.
If you decide to shoulder your bow and draw a hand weapon, turn to **251**.

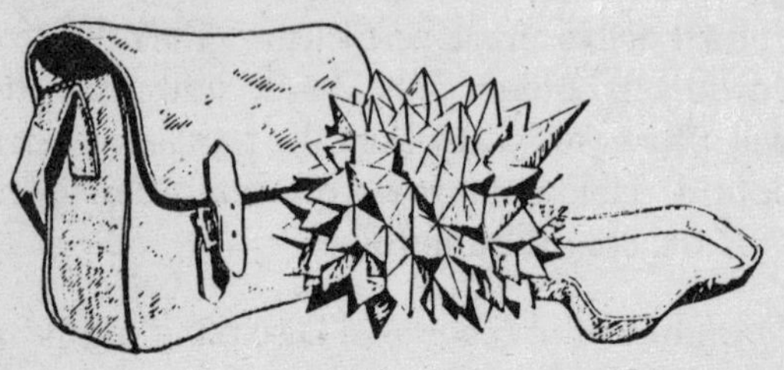

132

The men glare at you uncertainly. 'If you've come here to kill me,' says the pretender, 'you've come on a suicide mission.'

Slowly the five rise to their feet and step away from the fire, their hands drifting casually towards the hilts of their swords. On a whispered cue they unsheathe their blades and attack you.

Partisans: COMBAT SKILL 24 ENDURANCE 36

You can evade combat at any time; turn to **23**.
If you win the combat, turn to **170**.

133

You draw the Sommerswerd and hold the shimmering blade before your face. The phantoms give a ghastly shriek as its golden light scorches the unnatural fabric of their forms. Unused to the sensation of pain, they recoil but they do not disperse or abandon their attack. Their need to feed on your life-force overcomes their fear of your sword. With a terrifying howl of anger they swirl around you and swoop down to attack.

Cener Ghosts: COMBAT SKILL 32 ENDURANCE 40

These undead beings are immune to Mindblast (but not Psi-surge). Remember to double all ENDURANCE point losses sustained by the enemy due to the power of the Sommerswerd.

If you win the combat, turn to **156**.

134

You dig your heels into the flanks of your horse but he reacts sluggishly: his senses have been dulled by the heady aroma of the flowers and he has barely enough strength to canter. A whirring sound fills your ears and instinctively you flatten yourself against the horse's neck as the sound grows louder. A Bolas, three solid metal balls connected by strong cords tied together in the shape of a letter 'Y', skims your scalp and smashes into the base of the gorge. Frantically you urge your horse onwards, but he stumbles and his forelegs buckle beneath him. You are thrown forward and concussed as your head hits the ground: lose 3 ENDURANCE points.

If you possess a Bullwhip, turn to **214**.
If you do not have this Special Item, turn to **327**.

135

Inch by inch you climb the sheer rock wall, transferring your weight from one hollow to the next with painstaking care. The higher you climb, the more you have to support yourself solely with your fingers until, at last, you reach up and take hold of a trailing mass of tree roots, which are strong enough to hold your weight. With great effort you haul yourself out of the chasm and collapse into the undergrowth: lose 3 ENDURANCE points.

As soon as your strength returns, you check your equipment and advance deeper into the eerie forest.

Turn to **50**.

136

The Death Knights tramp past your hiding place and hurry out of the chamber. Paido breathes a sigh of relief as the sound of their heavy footfalls is quickly lost in the noise of the alarm bell; but only when you are sure you are alone do you leave your hiding place and approach the triangular doors.

Turn to **230**.

137

On the hill the Drakkarim are beginning to falter; they are no match for the Palace Guard, the cream of the Eruan army. As their casualties escalate their line crumbles and suddenly they turn to flee in disarray towards the town. An explosion rumbles across the field and a billowing cloud of black smoke rises from the temple. Your stomach churns and you fear the worst as smoke and debris pour from the ruins like an erupting volcano. Then, as quickly as it began, the eruption subsides and the smoke clears to reveal a triumphant Prince Graygor, clutching the Eruan flag and exhorting his troops to victory. The Palace Guard have captured the hill, and the sorcery that threatened to destroy them has been smashed. But from where you stand you can see a new threat fast approaching the Prince and his men, a threat that could kill them all.

Turn to **270**.

138

With breathtaking speed you clear the rampart and reach the stunned Adamas. Rocks continue to crash down but you ignore the danger as you drag the injured lord to safety with just one second to spare.

Turn to **301**.

139

You draw on your psychic energy and launch a pulse of psi-power at his mind. He staggers backwards, his mailed fists clenched to the sides of his black helm as your attack rakes his nervous system. But he is inured to pain. His years of training in the combat pits of

Blackshroud have tempered his nerves so that he can withstand agonies that would destroy an ordinary man. He regains his balance and raises his spear to strike.

If you wish to stand and fight this warrior, turn to **180**.
If you choose to evade combat, turn to **316**.

140

After a week of trekking across difficult terrain, the firm surface of the hill track feels as smooth as a mirror beneath your aching feet. By noon you have put ten miles behind you, and have reached a bridge which crosses a sickly yellow stream flowing down from the surrounding hills. You must now eat a Meal or lose 3 ENDURANCE points.

You are about to continue your journey across the bridge when you hear a rumble of hoofbeats and see a group of horsemen, shrouded in dust, riding along the road towards you.

If you have the Magnakai Discipline of Huntmastery and have reached the rank of Principalin or more, turn to **12**.
If you do not possess this skill, or have yet to reach this level of Kai training, you can either wait for these riders to reach you; turn to **122**.
Or hide beneath the bridge; turn to **322**.

141

The bore-hole is cramped and you can progress only by crawling along on your hands and knees. A gentle breeze stirs the dust at the base of the shaft and a faint glow in the distance sheds just enough light for you to be able to see your way ahead. Gradually the slope becomes steeper and you are forced to climb a crude staircase formed by jagged outcrops of rock. Above you see a strip of daylight and it draws you upward with its promise of escape.

As you climb nearer to the opening you hear a hissing sound off to your right. Instantly you freeze as you catch sight of a black serpent, its jaw open and its venomous fangs glinting in the gloom of a hollow. It is coiled upon a nest of eggs less than an arm's length from your face.

If you have the Magnakai Discipline of Animal Control, turn to **35**.
If you wish to ignore the snake and continue your climb, turn to **235**.
If you decide to retreat along the bore-hole and attempt to climb the chasm wall instead, turn to **135**.

142

It takes several minutes to pick the lock using your dagger, and in doing so you snap the tip off and ruin the blade: delete this weapon from your *Action Chart*.

The door opens on to a passageway lined with torches. Half-way along the left wall you see another door – a solid slab of iron broken only by a small, barred window. Silently you approach it and peer in through the grille.

If you have visited the Danarg in a previous Lone Wolf adventure, turn to **260**.
If not, turn to **114**.

143

The warrior stoops to snatch up the shimmering rod but the Prince leaps forward and kicks it from his grasp. His action costs him dearly, for when his foot touches the stave a blast of searing flame scorches his leg and hurls him backwards to the ground. You rush forward and block the warrior's attempt to scurry after his weapon. Cursing vilely, he snatches a dagger from his belt and launches himself at your throat.

Ziran: COMBAT SKILL 25 ENDURANCE 33

If you win the combat, turn to **56**.

144

That night you make camp in a stone hut. It is little better than a hovel but at least it provides shelter from the rain, which begins to fall shortly after dark and is still falling when you set off again at dawn. The dull grey hours pass uneventfully until the wooded shoreline gradually gives way to a wilderness of slime-laden mud flats and twisted, petrified trees. Here the current is weak and you are forced to row in order to make progress through the brown, scum-flecked water. Jarel sits at the prow, his wolfskin cloak drawn close around his shoulders to keep out the chill rain. He stares fixedly ahead as he guides you through the narrow channels that bisect this evil-smelling swamp. Twice you find yourselves caught in watery cul-de-sacs and have to retrace your course, but as the light begins to fade you catch sight of an island that promises firm mooring and a place to camp overnight.

Pick a number from the *Random Number Table*.

If the number you have picked is *0–4*, turn to **59**. If it is *5–9*, turn to **259**.

145

Halgar falls heavily to his knees, the blood oozing thickly between his fingers as life deserts him. With a gurgling croak he stiffens and drops sideways into the fire, smothering the embers and filling the air with the smell of scorched leather. At your feet lies the cruelly fashioned Bullwhip, and nearby you discover a backpack. Flicking open the buckle, you tip the contents out on to the grimy stone floor. The pack contains the following items:

LEATHER POUCH CONTAINING 36 LUNE (9 Gold Crowns)
TORCH
TINDER BOX
BOTTLE OF WATER

You may keep any or all of these items. If you decide to keep the Bullwhip, mark it on your *Action Chart* as a Special Item.

Set into the floor you discover a wooden trapdoor that gives access to an empty cellar. You hide the body in the cellar before remounting your horse, crossing the bridge and continuing your ride to Pirsi.

Turn to **75**.

146

The smell of their blood makes your stomach heave, but your grim labour does not go unrewarded. Inside the bushes you discover their catch of fish. There are enough speckled trout here for 5 Meals. It you take any of the fish remember to record them on your *Action Chart*.

To cross the river and continue, turn to **335**.

147

With terrifying ease the Demonlord throws open the stone door, which splits asunder as it slams against the temple wall. You release your arrow and send it burrowing deep into the creature's chest. The Demonlord laughs mockingly and plucks the shaft from his body as if it were no more of an irritation than a tiny splinter. No blood oozes from the wound and the puncture seals itself quickly to leave no mark on the creamy skin of the supernatural creature.

'Surrender yourself, mortal!' he commands. 'And I shall spare you the agonies of death.'

If you possess the Sommerswerd, turn to **286**.
If you do not possess this Special Item, turn to **333**.

148 – *Illustration IX*

Both you and the Lencian officer, whose name is Captain Prarg, ride back and forth, rallying the few soldiers left to support the hard-pressed knights locked in battle at the bridge. A motley company of cross-bowmen, halberdiers, wounded men-at-arms, wagon drivers, cooks, heralds and battle-shocked pikemen are finally assembled, and they march forward with their shields raised and their weapons poised.

On your left, the Prince's reserves respond to a signal from the hill and advance to support their leader. On your right, massed ranks of Lencian spearmen are locked in pitched combat the length of the orchard

IX. A Drakkarim Death Knight draws back his weapon and prepares to strike at your neck

wall. As you near the bridge you encounter the bodies of those slain by the crackling rays of electric fire. The sight of their tortured forms, weapons fused in their lifeless hands, sends a wave of shock through your company. 'Forward men!' shouts Captain Prarg. 'Raise your eyes and advance!'

The bridge looms out of the battle smoke ahead and your men surge towards the macabre struggle taking place. The bodies of the dead lie six deep, covering the whole area of the approach and filling the ditch on either side. War-cries roar with harsh anger and the air is alive with the clangour of striking steel and the howl of violent death.

'Charge!' you shout, and the company pours across the bridge. Reinforced by fresh troops, the knights finally break through the barricade and into the streets beyond. The struggle grows ever more intense as the Drakkarim defenders throw themselves into the fray with total disregard for their lives. One such defender, an elite Drakkarim Death Knight, hacks his way through the leading pikemen and slays your horse with one terrible blow of his two-handed axe. As you fall, he draws back his weapon, its razor-sharp blade trailing scarlet spray, and prepares to strike at your neck.

Death Knight: COMBAT SKILL 24 ENDURANCE 40

Owing to his state of battle frenzy, your enemy is immune to Mindblast (but not Psi-surge).

If you win the combat turn to **206**.

149

Your arrow grazes one of the magicians and thuds into

the shield of a Drakkarim warrior standing behind him. The wound is superficial and it does not prevent the magician from hurling his sphere at the Palmyrions.

Turn to **106**.

150

The foot knights of Lencia are the first to go forward, their densely packed columns marching in perfect order towards the bridge at the centre of the enemy line. As they come within range there is a sound like rushing water and a cloud of black arrows pours down on their armoured ranks. Huge gaps appear in the line and the columns seem to sway under the impact before continuing the assault. They are flanked to the south by crossbowmen, who are firing their weapons as they advance. Unlike the knights, they wear very little armour and over half their number are felled by arrows when they halt to reload their cumbersome bows. The survivors retreat, taking cover among the massed ranks of Lencian spearmen who are advancing towards the orchard.

Prince Graygor signals to his pikemen and men-at-arms to support the Lencian knights, who are engaged in a bitter hand-to-hand fight at the stone bridge. They are within 100 yards of the bridge when a crackling ray of electric fire sweeps down from the ruins of the temple. It rips through their packed ranks with devastating effect, blasting the pikemen high into the air.

If you have the Magnakai Discipline of Divination and have reached the rank of Tutelary or more, turn to **323**.

(continued over)

If you have the Magnakai Discipline of Huntmastery and have reached the rank of Principalin or more turn to **258**.

If you have neither of these skills, or have yet to reach these levels of Kai training, turn to **42**.

151

The officer shrugs his shoulders and climbs back on to his horse. 'He's probably an outlaw or a deserter from the Eruan army,' he says to his men. 'Either way we must ride on; we've wasted too much time here already.'

He spurs his horse forward and you are forced to leap aside as the riders surge across the bridge and disappear along the road that leads to the Moggador Forest.

Turn to **179**.

152

The captain nods to the owner. You hear a click followed by a rush of air as the crossbow bolt hurtles towards your back. Your senses scream a warning and you respond by hurling yourself on to the floor. A look of terror barely has time to register on the captain's face before the speeding missile embeds itself between his startled eyes.

'Get him!' shouts the owner, and three stocky drinkers rush forward with short swords held ready to strike. The first attacker loses his sword and the hand that holds it. As he reels back, screaming, the others exchange a fearful glance and halt in their tracks.

If you wish to advance and attack them, turn to **274**.

If you wish to try to escape from the log tavern, turn to **68**.

153

The arrows screech past on all sides but your lightning reactions save you and your mount from their merciless bite. You dig in your heels, urging your horse on towards the ford, but as you are about to enter the shallows an arrow buries itself deep in your horse's neck. He shrieks in pain and crashes to his knees, hurling you into the river. You gulp a mouthful of the icy water and struggle to your feet, coughing and cursing, just in time to see your ambushers pour out of the nearest hut and advance towards you. Some are reloading their bows as they run.

If you have a bow and wish to use it, turn to **131**.
If you wish to try to escape by wading across the ford, turn to **166**.
If you wish to draw a hand weapon and prepare for combat, turn to **251**.

154

You land with a jolt at the edge of the chasm, but the soil is dry and flaky and disintegrates on impact. Frantically you make a grab for a tangle of roots and hold fast as your legs swing wildly in the void. But the weight and violent movement of your body proves more than the roots can withstand. They tear loose and you tumble backwards into the chasm.

Turn to **257**.

155

You reach a square near the centre of the town where a unit of enemy reserves are gathered, awaiting the order to join the battle. They are Krorn – hideous-looking creatures from the Moggador and Akamazim forests. They are approached by a swarthy giant of a man, with a short black beard and shiny bald head, who brandishes a massive war-axe fashioned from a fiery red metal. The axe must weigh more that its wielder but he waves it above his head as if it were no heavier than a stick of wood. Judging from his features and from what you have heard during your travels through Eru, this warrior is Baron Shinzar – the enemy commander.

If you have a bow and wish to use it, turn to **96**.
If not, turn to **73**.

156

A sudden calm descends on the surrounding forest as the last of the ghosts is dispelled by your attack. But the silence is soon shattered by a chilling howl that comes from somewhere deep beneath the ground. Shaken by your encounter and anxious to avoid further conflict with the evil spirits of this isle, you enter the forest and hurry away towards the east.

Turn to **175**.

157

Your senses tell you that the man is lying: he is not

the partisan leader. He repeats the question but still you hesitate to answer. You cast your eyes over each man in turn and your senses confirm your suspicions: none of these men is Sebb Jarel.

If you wish to ask the mouse-like man why he is lying, turn to **51**.
If you wish to draw a weapon and challenge him to prove his identity, turn to **132**.
If you wish to leave the cave, turn to **23**.

158

The warrior lord looks at you reproachfully, and from a pocket of his surcoat he takes out a glittering gem. 'The Elder Magi of Dessi have bestowed upon us generous gifts to aid our fight against the Darklands,' he says, holding the gem in the palm of his hand. Then he breathes the words of an incantation and green flames dance wildly around the sparkling jewel.

If you have the Magnakai Discipline of Psi-shield, turn to **262**.
If you do not possess this skill, turn to **64**.

159

'Just as I thought,' says the sergeant, anger in his voice. 'This is Halgar's whip. And judging by these bloodstains I'd wager he didn't part with it gladly.'

On hearing this, the other partisans reach for their swords and you catch the glint of murder in their eyes. You begin to explain but they refuse to listen. Instead they unsheathe their blades and encircle you slowly. (Delete the Bullwhip from your list of Special Items.)

If you wish to evade combat, turn to **39**.

(continued over)

If you wish to stand your ground and fight them, turn to **118**.

160

You sense that the crystal rods are generating a powerful charge of negative energy. The Lorestones are being bombarded with this energy in the hope that eventually it will destroy them. If you are to retrieve the Lorestones safely you must first shut off this power. However, by doing so, you would remove the means by which they are being kept suspended in the air, and they would then fall into the pit.

You ponder the problem for several minutes before you hit upon a solution.

Turn to **5**.

161

Using your much improved Kai skills, you disappear into the forest, leaving no trace of your passing. Even the smell of your blood is masked by your ability to secrete neutralizing oils through the pores of your skin which act as a chemical camouflage.

Turn to **268**.

162

As the last of the Death Knights falls dead at your feet, you clamber over the corpses and run towards the stairs. Paido arms himself with a Drakkar sword and follows as you pound up the steps towards the two triangular doors.

Turn to **230**.

163

Majestically the Palace Guard advance across the field of battle, their lances raised like the spines of a steel porcupine, their scarlet and yellow pennons streaming behind them in the wind. The enemy shower them with a rain of arrows, yet the Eruans seemingly ignore these deadly shafts and continue undeterred. It is not until they reach the ditch that the constant bowfire begins to abrade their ranks. However, it does little to slow their pace as the Prince gives the order to charge. The knights level their lances as they reach the bottom of the hill. Above them a regiment of Drakkarim pikemen brace themselves to receive the attack and a blaze of lightning hurtles down from the temple wall. You wince as it streaks down the hill, but miraculously it misses its intended target and explodes near the ditch, hurling nothing but scorched mud and the bodies of those already slain into the sky.

The Prince's battle-cry rings out and his knights slam into the Drakkarim to break like a wave against their wall of pikes. The Prince and a small group of his stoutest guardsmen break through and gallop on towards the temple whilst the remaining knights engage in fierce hand-to-hand combat. The Prince and his group reach the temple and you see them dismount and enter the ruins. Such bravery stirs your admiration, for they know the deadly danger that lurks there, yet they confront it unflinchingly.

Turn to **137**.

164

Your arrow screams towards a magician and shatters the sphere clasped in his claw-like hand. There is a brilliant flash as it explodes, scattering fragments that hiss like a host of fiery snakes among the Drakkarim. The second magician drops his sphere setting off another explosion. The Drakkarim scream in pain and terror as the fragments burn everything they touch.

Turn to **332**.

165

You muster all your willpower and strength to drag yourself from under your dead horse and, after clawing the muck from your eyes, you crawl along the ditch. Just ahead you see a Palace Guard in a similar predicament to yourself. However, not only is he pinned beneath his dead mount, but his head is buried in the mud and he is slowly suffocating to death. He is thrashing his arms wildly in desperation.

If you wish to save his life by pulling him out from beneath his horse, turn to **79**.
If you prefer to ignore his plight and look instead for a new horse, turn to **247**.
If you decide to climb out of the ditch and follow the Prince's attack on foot, turn to **115**.

166

The water laps at your waist as you wade through the shallows, and the shouts and howls of your ambushers ring relentlessly in your ears. Arrows splash beside you or whistle past dangerously close. You are three-quarters of the way across when one shaft clips your neck and knocks you underwater.

Pick a number from the *Random Number Table* (*0–10*). If you have the Magnakai Discipline of Huntmastery, deduct 2 from the number you have picked. The resulting figure equals the number of ENDURANCE points lost as a result of the wound.

If you survive the wounding, you reach the opposite shore and escape into the Moggador Forest on foot.

Turn to **186**.

167

You slump forward in the saddle, your eyelids half closed, your body possessed of a creeping fatigue that robs you of all will to resist the potent scent. The vibrant colours swirl before your eyes and then fade as gradually you lose consciousness and tumble to the ground.

If you possess a Bullwhip, turn to **214**.
If you do not have this Special Item, turn to **327**.

168

The tiny nuggets of copper woven into the braids of the Bullwhip begin to glow with a strange yellow light.

You tug it free from your pack and the phantoms give a ghastly shriek as the yellow rays scorch their unnatural forms. Unused to the sensation of pain, they recoil and take shelter in the shadows.

The presence of the phantoms has triggered a spell that was cast upon the whip long ago by a former owner. Whenever the Bullwhip comes into contact with undead beings, it protects its owner by radiating a power that is abhorrent to them.

The phantoms retreat but they do not disperse or abandon their attack. Their need to feed on your life-force overcomes their fear of the whip and with a terrifying howl of anger they swoop out of the trees and strike.

Cener Ghosts: COMBAT SKILL 24 ENDURANCE 40

These creatures are immune to Mindblast (but not Psi-surge). Owing to the power of the whip, add 2 points to your COMBAT SKILL for the duration of the combat.

If you win the fight, turn to **156**.

169

The water around the boat is stained a sickly green with the blood of the Ciquali that you have slain. However, two of the creatures have survived your murderous counter-attack and have slunk beneath the bow. Suddenly there is a loud crack as a sharpened wooden stake rips through the timbers close by your feet, and a fountain of water gushes from the hole. The boat tilts violently and both you and Jarel are pitched headlong into the murky river.

With the blood-stained water stinging your eyes, you strike out blindly in the hope of reaching the bank before you fall foul of your attackers. Cold and shaken, you eventually reach the south bank and drag yourself on to the muddy shore.

Turn to **226**.

170

The last of your attackers screams and falls backwards into the fire, smothering the flames and plunging the cavern into darkness. Seconds later the curtain that covers the entrance is whipped aside and in stride two partisan guards, their spears poised ready to thrust. They are blinded by the unexpected darkness and you have no difficulty slipping past them and escaping along the passage.

At the exit from the cave you notice a patrol of partisan horsemen arriving at the camp. They dismount, tether their horses to some bushes and walk wearily towards the main campfire. Seeing an opportunity to escape, you rush towards the bushes and snatch the reins of the nearest mount. Suddenly a cry echoes from the cave: the guards are raising the alarm. You climb into the saddle but your escape is blocked by a partisan horseman who is riding up the narrow track that leads into the camp.

Partisan Horseman:
COMBAT SKILL 17 ENDURANCE 24

If you win the combat, turn to **239**.

171

'I cannot send him,' says the Prince, uncomfortably. 'He is needed elsewhere. We must send another to gather the information we need.'

The King looks displeased but rather than argue with his ally on the eve of battle, he sends instead for one of his horse scouts. The Prince breathes a quiet sigh of relief before ordering you to return to his headquarters.

Turn to **29**.

172 – *Illustration X*

As the lumbering reptile draws near, your first reaction is to run for the safety of the stone hut, but you are prevented from doing so by the sticky, knee-deep mud. The scaly creature raises its horned snout and emits a long, croaking growl as the scent of fear wafts towards it on the breeze. Jarel unsheathes his sword and moves to your side as the monster begins its attack.

Gorodon: COMBAT SKILL 29 ENDURANCE 36

Halve any ENDURANCE losses you sustain during this combat as half of the creature's attacks are directed at Jarel.

If you win the combat, turn to **217**.

173

Just as you catch up with your men, a mass of leather-clad Hammerlanders emerge from the cottages, rending the air with their howling battle-cries. They strike from every side, catching you like helpless fish in a barrel.

If you wish to stand and fight your attackers, turn to **288**.

If you wish to try to escape from this ambush, turn to **16**.

X. The scaly Gorodon lumbers towards you

174

Long, curved talons extend from his hairless paws and with terrifying ease he throws open the stone door, which splits asunder as it slams against the temple wall.

'Surrender yourself, mortal!' he commands, his eyes glowing with a supernatural fire. 'And I shall spare you the agonies of death.'

If you possess the Sommerswerd, turn to **286**.
If you do not possess this Special Item, turn to **333**.

175

For two hours you stumble through the forest until fatigue finally catches up with you. Exhausted, you stop and crouch down, with your back against the trunk of a gnarled pine and your knees drawn up to your chin (you must now eat a Meal or lose 3 ENDURANCE points). Unable to resist any longer, you close your eyes and drift off into a deep sleep.

Turn to **295**.

176

Before leaving Luomi, the Prince gives you a Signet Ring that bears his royal crest (mark this as a Special Item on your *Action Chart*; you need not discard another Special Item in favour of this ring if you already carry the maximum of twelve items). By wearing the ring on your right hand you signify that you have the friendship of the royal court, something that may prove valuable when trying to persuade Sebb Jarel to aid you in your quest.

You exchange farewells with Prince Graygor, before checking your equipment and setting off on the dusty road to Pirsi. The road itself is little better than a dirt track that cuts across open grassland towards a wide, muddy river. Awkward heaps of grey stone dot the unkempt landscape: they are the deserted ruins of farmsteads and houses destroyed during the Drakkarim occupation.

After an hour in the saddle you arrive at the river at a point where a wide stone bridge spans its murky waters. A fire-blackened watchtower and a roofless stone hut stand at the approach to the bridge. You notice a faint wisp of woodsmoke rising from the top of the tower and a saddled horse grazing close by at the river's edge.

If you wish to stop and investigate the watchtower, turn to **232**.

If you prefer to cross the bridge and continue, turn to **75**.

177

His body rolls down the stairs and comes to rest in an undignified heap near the bottom. You are loath to touch him but he may possess some useful items. Gritting your teeth you pull him over on to his back, empty his pockets and discover the following items:

BLACK KEY (Backpack Item)
200 KIKA (20 Gold Crowns)
DAGGER

You may take whatever items you wish but remember to adjust your *Action Chart* accordingly.

To continue your exploration, turn to **285**.

178

Your blow is strong and deadly accurate. It lays open the wolf's chest and cleaves its heart in two, sending the beast crashing into the dense undergrowth amid the spray of its own foul blood.

Breathless with exertion and fearful of what may still be lurking unseen in the shadows, you gather up your equipment and follow Jarel. He is anxious to get away from the dead wolves before the smell of their blood attracts more of their kind, or worse.

Turn to **282**.

179

The road winds upwards through the arid hills until it reaches a ridge of yellow rock. You climb to the crest of the ridge and catch your first awe-inspiring glimpse of Torgar.

The walls of this grim city-fortress stand upon the brink of a ravine cut deep by centuries of rushing water. A natural causeway of stone spans the dark chasm and provides the only means of approaching Torgar from the south. It has an enviable position and its defences seem impregnable. It commands the only road into the barren land of Ghatan, and any who dare travel that road must pass over the causeway and through the city's great iron gate.

In the past there have been few who would venture willingly to Torgar, but now the causeway and its approaches swarm with such men. They are the soldiers of Talestria and Palmyrion, and they have come with their engines of war to lay siege to this grim Drakkar fortress.

Less than a mile from the ridge stands a cluster of tents, perched on top of a hillock which overlooks the siege-works. As you approach them a group of knights appears from the largest tent and command you to halt. One of them, an officer, recognizes the uniform you wear and bids you enter the tent to meet his commander. All of the knights are armed and you decide it prudent not to refuse the officer's request.

If you have ever visited the land of Talestria in a previous Lone Wolf adventure, turn to **45**.
If not, turn to **346**.

180

You leap from the shadows and aim a mighty blow at the Death Knight's head. But in spite of the speed of your attack and the encumbrance of his heavy armour, the warrior manages to turn aside your blow with the tip of his spear.

Death Knight: COMBAT SKILL 24 ENDURANCE 38

The warrior is immune to Mindblast (but not Psi-surge).

If you win the fight in two rounds or less, turn to **316**.
If you win the fight in three rounds or more, turn to **261**.

181

The track consists of ancient paving blocks mostly overgrown with moss, but occasionally you hear the sound of a distant hoofbeat striking upon an exposed slab of stone. You follow the trail and are soon engulfed by darkness. Only the sound of forest owls and the flutter of bats can be heard as you make your way slowly through the inky-black forest.

You have been walking less than an hour when you arrive at a stone bridge. The stream it once crossed has long since dried up, and the empty water-course is blanketed with dead leaves. You are now very tired and in need of food and rest.

If you wish to stop and rest here at the bridge, turn to **204**.

If you decide to forego rest and continue along the track, turn to **37**.

182

A sharp pain lances through your neck and shoulder as the serpent sinks its fangs into the side of your throat. It thrashes wildly but you manage to grip it behind its head, prise it loose from your flesh and fling it down the bore-hole. A sudden wave of nausea leaves you shaking with fear as the deadly venom begins to take effect.

If you have the Magnakai Discipline of Curing and have reached the rank of Mentora, turn to **192**.

If you have the Magnakai Discipline of Curing and have reached the rank of Primate, turn to **246**.

If you do not possess this skill, or have yet to attain either of these levels of Kai training, turn to **343**.

183

You land with a splash and roll into the ditch to avoid being trampled by the following horses. After clawing the muck from your eyes, you crawl along the channel. A short distance ahead of you a knight is pinned beneath his dead horse. He is flailing his arms wildly and you can see that his head is trapped beneath the mud and he is slowly drowning.

If you wish to save his life by pulling him out from beneath his horse, turn to **79**.

If you choose to ignore his plight, you can remount your own horse; turn to **334**.

Or you can follow the Prince's attack on foot; turn to **115**.

184

The yells of the Drakkarim echo along the battlements as they watch you sprinting towards the city. Then a rain of boulders slams down with terrific force, spraying you with splinters of stone as they disintegrate on impact. Your senses keep you safe as instinctively you dodge the falling rocks and then skid to a halt in front of the door. You plant and prime the crystal explosive, and run back, counting the seconds with every step. You clear the rampart on the count of seven and flatten yourself behind its protective wall.

Turn to **301**.

185

At your approach, one of the partisan horsemen points at the Bullwhip fastened to your backpack and says something to his sergeant.

'That's a fine whip you have there, Pathfinder,' says the sergeant, as you bring your horse to a halt. 'I admire good craftsmanship. Would you mind if I examined it more closely?'

If you wish to show the sergeant your Bullwhip, turn to **159**.

If you refuse to let him examine it, turn to **198**.

If you have the Magnakai Discipline of Divination and wish to use it, turn to **302**.

186

The ground rises steeply and it is dusk before your climb ends at the crest of a ridge overlooking the grasslands of Northern Eru. In less than an hour it will be dark, so you decide to camp here on the ridge and continue at first light (you must now eat a meal or lose 3 ENDURANCE points).

You are settling down on a mattress of leaf mould when the howl of a timber wolf prompts you to abandon your soft bed and spend the night in the bough of a tree.

Turn to **125**.

187 – *Illustration XI*

You unsheathe a hand weapon and crouch in readiness to receive the creature's attack. It howls, almost with glee, as it anticipates sinking its great yellow fangs into your unprotected throat.

Taintor Wolf: COMBAT SKILL 27 ENDURANCE 49

If you win and the fight last for four rounds or less, turn to **202**.

If the fight lasts longer than four rounds, do not continue but instead turn to **234**.

188

Mustering your strength and your psychic defences, you concentrate on repelling Roark's attack. Immediately, the icy chill that threatens to freeze your heart begins to thaw, and you feel warmth flowing along your arm towards the iron amulet clenched in your fist. Suddenly Roark screams with pain and collapses – he has fallen victim to his own attack. You have reversed the flow of energy and stopped his heart.

XI. The Taintor Wolf howls as it anticipates sinking its great yellow fangs into your unprotected throat

189

Using this energy, you turn to confront Tagazin. He shudders as your psychic commands rob him of his supernatural strength. His body becomes pale, almost transparent, and wisps of smoke curl from his skin as if his body were slowly evaporating. He retreats towards the centre of the temple and leaps on to the marble block. There is a chilling howl and suddenly the shadowy chamber is flooded with blinding light. Thunder booms and the walls shake. Terrified, Roark's followers flee through the shattered doors and scramble up the stairs. Crackling bolts of white lightning leap from the block to tear chunks of rock from the temple walls, and the air seethes with a cloying stench that threatens to suffocate you. With terror in your heart you bound up the steps and escape as the defeated spirit of the Demonlord vents its spite in the chamber below.

Turn to **341**.

189

'Naog daka!' snarls a voice in the corridor behind. You spin round to see two Drakkarim warriors, both armed with loaded crossbows. Slowly you let your hand drift towards your weapon but your move does not go unnoticed. Suddenly a starburst of pain explodes in your head and darkness washes over your vision as you are slammed back against the door by the force of the bolt which has penetrated your skull. Death is instantaneous.

Your life and your quest end here.

190

You are lucky that the arrows that pierced your back were neither barbed nor tipped with poison. You grit your teeth, muster your remaining strength and stagger to your feet.

Fifty yards from the allies' picket line you see two Lencian men-at-arms moving towards you with their swords drawn. 'Give the password!' they command. 'Give the password or perish!'

If you wish to answer, 'Shortsword', turn to **63.**
If you wish to answer, 'Broadsword', turn to **227**.
If you wish to answer, 'Longsword', turn to **347**.

191

Your Kai mastery alerts you to a deadly danger. The boat is being held from beneath by a group of amphibian creatures who intend to launch a surprise attack. You warn Jarel of what you sense and quietly you both unsheathe your weapons in readiness to receive their attack.

Turn to **245**.

192

You draw on your inner strength to overcome the venom that is coursing through your veins. The deadly neuro-vascular poison is swiftly neutralized, but at a cost to you of 3 ENDURANCE points.

Make the necessary adjustment to your *Action Chart* and turn to **205**.

193

'Imposter!' bellows the captain, and lunges forward

to grab you by the throat. But you sidestep his attack deftly and strike a blow to his temple with the heel of your palm that renders him unconscious in an instant.

'Fire!' shouts a bull-necked Pirsian, and you throw yourself to the ground. A deafening roar reverberates through the town as the men discharge their unwieldy pistols, but the lead shot passes harmlessly over your head and buries itself in the tavern door. The noise stirs a hornet's nest of activity as the townsfolk arm themselves and rush into the street to investigate the commotion. The situation looks desperate, but you can see a chance to escape and you take it. The pistols created a huge cloud of white smoke and under cover of this acrid cloud you scurry down an alley beside the log tavern and leap headlong into the foliage and trees beyond.

With the angry shouts of the villagers rippling through the forest, you curse your ill luck as you escape into the darkness.

Turn to **250**.

194

You recognize the language being spoken by the owners of the harsh voices – it is Krorn. A shiver runs down your spine when you recall what you have heard about the evil creatures who speak this tongue, how they delight in cruelty and love nothing better than to devour human flesh. It would be wise to avoid them, but in order to reach the ford you have to pass close by the bushes. From what little you can hear of their conversation, they are arguing over some fish they have caught. As you creep nearer you pray that their argument will keep them distracted long enough for you to reach the river unseen.

Pick a number from the *Random Number Table*. If you have completed the Lore-circle of Solaris, add 3 to the number you have picked.

If your total is now 6 or less, turn to **67**.
If it is 7 or more, turn to **335**.

195

You see the wolf cringe as your arrow sinks feather-deep into its throat. It opens its great jaw but no howl escapes from its frightful, fang-filled mouth as it crashes nose-first into the soft forest earth, somersaults and rolls limply to a halt at your feet.

Turn to **202**.

196

As each rod is broken its beam disappears and the fireball grows weaker. The golden light of the Lorestones begins to radiate through the evil green flames, and when Paido has destroyed half the rods, one of them tips and falls into your waiting hands. Immediately, a wave of energy courses through your body, filling you with renewed strength and sharpening your thoughts and perceptions. You shout encouragement to your companion and he raises his head to reply, but his words are drowned by a harsh and terrible voice.

Turn to **350**.

197

You mount your horse and set off towards King Sarnac's headquarters at a gallop. On your ride you pass the survivors of the regiment who were blasted at the bridge. Deeply shocked they stand in groups or cower on the ground like frightened animals. The horror on their faces and the sound of their whimpering sickens your heart.

As you cross the road and climb towards the King's tent, a Lencian cavalry officer comes riding down the hill towards you. He seems to recognize you and he calls for you to stop.

If you wish to bring your horse to a halt and find out what he wants, turn to **105**.
If you choose to ignore his signal and continue your ride to King Sarnac's headquarters, turn to **21**.

198

'Pah!' spits the sergeant, accusingly. 'Just as I thought. That's Halgar's whip you have – there's no other like it. I'd wager he didn't part with it gladly.'

On hearing this, the others reach for their swords and you catch the unmistakeable glint of murder in their eyes. You begin to explain but they refuse to listen. Instead they unsheathe their blades and begin to encircle you.

If you wish to evade combat, turn to **39**.
If you wish to stand and fight them, turn to **118**.

199

The Palmyrions are eager to attack the Drakkarim and rush forward, heedless of your warnings. The two robed figures draw back their arms and hurl the spheres at the onrushing soldiers. They hit and shatter with devastating effect.

Turn to **106**.

200

Behind the black door lies a vast temple lit by a ghastly green glow, which radiates from columns of crystal that rise from the floor and ascend into the dark reaches above. Near the centre of the room sits a giant block of sculptured marble and around it stands a group of hooded men, their faces hidden behind hideous masks of glass. The dismal sound of their chanting fills the chamber and, as their leader steps forward and removes his mask, so their voices rise in pitch and fervour.

If you have travelled the Stornlands of Central Magnamund in a previous Lone Wolf adventure, turn to **104**.
If you have never been to the Stornlands, turn to **263**.

201

You walk around the pit and soon realize that if you are to retrieve the Lorestones safely you must shut off the energy which is bombarding them. However, by doing so, you would remove the means by which they are being kept suspended in the air, and they would then fall into the pit.

You ponder the problem for several minutes before you hit upon a solution.

Turn to **5**.

202

Quickly you step away from the dead wolf and steel yourself as Jarel cries a warning: 'There's another one!'

There is a brief flash of feral eyes then the great hound charges out of the darkness and flings itself at your companion's chest. Jarel sidesteps and ducks, and the howling wolf meets with a swift death as Jarel's sword slices upwards and opens its heart.

Breathless and blood-splattered, you gather up your equipment and hurry deeper into the forest before the smell of the dead wolves attracts more of their kind, or worse.

Turn to **282**.

203

Despite the agony of your wounds you rise to your feet and stagger on towards the allies' camp. The arrows tear open your wounds with every jolting step you take and the terrible pain is too much to bear. With consciousness fading, you drop to your knees. The only hope you have of surviving is if you can wrench the arrows free.

Pick a number from the *Random Number Table*. If you have the Magnakai Discipline of Curing, deduct 3 from the number you have picked. The remaining number equals the number of additional ENDURANCE points you lose as a result of pulling the arrows from your back.

If you survive the trauma of this action, turn to **190**.

204

Cautiously you investigate beneath the bridge, and to your relief discover that it is deserted. You are hungry and exhausted after your ordeal and must now eat a Meal or lose 3 ENDURANCE points. Too tired to continue, you settle down on the soft mattress of leaves and drift off into a deep sleep.

Turn to **295**.

205

You claw your way out of the bore-hole and collapse on to the damp earth that surrounds the fissure. As your energy returns, you pull yourself to your feet and try to get your bearings before venturing deeper into the eerie forest.

Your wounds and the energy expended during your ordeal in the chasm have sapped your strength. You must now eat a Meal or lose 3 ENDURANCE points.

Turn to **50**.

206

All around you the battle rages. Having lost the bridge,

the Drakkarim draw together in desperate groups and attempt to throw barricades across the narrow street. While Captain Prarg rallies the pikemen and leads an attack along the main street in an effort to break through one of these hastily built defences, you gather about you a score of men and enter an alley to your left in pursuit of a handful of retreating Drakkarim Death Knights.

If you possess the Magnakai Discipline of Pathsmanship and have reached the rank of Tutelary or more, turn to **225**.

If you do not possess this skill or have yet to reach this level of training, turn to **345**.

207

Slowly he drags himself to his feet and stumbles drunkenly towards the rampart. You shout encouragement, then suddenly a starburst of pain explodes in your head and the taste of blood fills your mouth: you have been struck in the face by a Drakkarim arrow. It has pierced your eye and lodged itself in your brain. Death is instantaneous.

Your life and your quest end here.

208 – *Illustration XII*

Instinctively you dodge aside, but the dagger gouges your neck before embedding itself in the door behind: lose 2 ENDURANCE points. The man curses as he pulls free his studded leather Bullwhip and lashes out. With deadly accuracy the plaited whip snakes towards your throat.

Halgar: COMBAT SKILL 24 ENDURANCE 30

XII. The man curses as he pulls free his studded leather Bullwhip and lashes out

Owing to the speed of his attack you cannot make use of a bow or evade combat.

If you win the fight, turn to **145**.

209

You swop seats with Jarel and take up the oars. The flow is much stronger here at the river mouth, but you are rested and you row with a strength and determination that overcomes the current. You have travelled over ten miles upstream when the bow rams against a submerged obstruction. The boat is near the middle of the river and you can see no obvious hazards, such as shoals or mud banks, but it is stuck fast, and no matter how hard you row you cannot free it.

If you have the Magnakai Discipline of Pathsmanship and have reached the rank of Tutelary or more, turn to **191**.

If you do not possess this skill, or have yet to reach this level of Kai training, turn to **28**.

210

With a shout of rage, you leap forward and strike a blow that would decapitate a creature of flesh and blood. But Tagazin is no such creature. A shower of icy-blue sparks explode where you strike his neck and your weapon disintegrates into a thousand frozen fragments: lose 2 ENDURANCE points (and remember to delete this weapon from your *Action Chart*).

Laughing maniacally, Tagazin bares his sword-like fangs and closes in for the kill.

If you possess another weapon, you can attempt to cut the amulet from around his neck; turn to **128**.

If you decide to attack Roark and take the amulet he is holding, turn to **41**.

211

Using your innate Kai skill of healing, you tend to the Prince's wounded leg and he soon stirs to consciousness. The Palace Guard have captured the hill and their banner flutters overhead proudly proclaiming their victory and inspiring the Lencians who are fighting at the bridge.

The Prince orders that a signal be sent to his reserves, instructing them to advance without delay, for the enemy are rallying to counter-attack. Tensely you watch as a mass of leather-clad Hammerlanders, supported by a regiment of grim-faced Brigandi, advance up the hill. The Palace Guard link their shields and prepare to welcome the enemy with sharpened steel. Onward they come, their banners held high, their war horns filling the air with a noisy clangour. They surge forward and with a yell the front rank slams into the shield wall. Sword blades fly, striking sparks and drawing blood. Axes and maces fall with crushing blows. A knight falls dead at your side and his slayer hurls himself through the gap. He scrambles to his feet and attacks you with his reddened blade.

Hammerlander: COMBAT SKILL 24   ENDURANCE 31

Owing to his state of battle frenzy the Hammerlander is immune to Mindblast (but not Psi-surge).

If you win the combat, turn to **87**.

212

Lord Adamas opens his hand and the coin shows 'tails' – you have guessed correctly. 'Very well,' he says, unbuckling his cumbersome sword belt and shouldering the satchel which contains the crystal explosive. 'Wish me luck!'

He orders the vanguard to provide covering fire with their crossbows, then he clambers over the rampart and sprints towards the Torgar gate.

Pick a number from the *Random Number Table*.

If the number you have picked is *0–4*, turn to **221**.
If it is *5–9*, turn to **32**.

213

A numbing chill leaves you shivering uncontrollably as a surge of psychic energy rips into the fabric of your mind: lose 5 ENDURANCE points.

The attack soon passes but your fear grows as you watch the jackal-like Demonlord leap from the marble block and come bounding towards the door.

If you have a bow and wish to use it, turn to **147**. If not, turn to **174**.

214

High above, crouched in their hiding places around the rim of the gorge, a company of partisans watches you succumb to the aroma of the flowers. When they are sure that you are unconscious, their sergeant leaves his position and descends by rope into the gorge, his nose and mouth covered by a pad of Golta leaves to counter the intoxicating scent. He had intended to bundle you on to your horse and lead you from the gorge to where the mountain air would revive you, but on reaching your body his suspicions are aroused. The ring and uniform you wear indicate that you are a Pathfinder with a message from Prince Graygor, but the weapons you carry, and your fair hair and Northland features are not those of an elite Eruan soldier. He rolls you over on to your stomach and is horrified to discover Halgar's Bullwhip tied to your backpack, its copper-studded coils stained with his blood. He knows that Halgar would never have parted willingly with the weapon, for it had made him as respected a fighter as his brother, Sebb Jarel. Anger, fuelled by shock, stirs the sergeant to a fit of rage. He is convinced that you are a Drakkar, an assassin sent by Baron Shinzar to murder the brothers Jarel. With a cry of anguish he unsheathes his sword and delivers a fateful blow that commits you to everlasting sleep.

Your life and your quest end here.

215

The air rushes past your face as you propel yourself

across the yawning gap. Then, with a loud crash, you land on the other side among the roots and briars, and roll over to lessen the shock of impact. Barbed thorns graze your face and arms (lose 2 ENDURANCE points) but you have made it across the chasm successfully. As soon as you recover you check your equipment and advance deeper into the eerie forest.

Turn to **50**.

216

After hearing who you are and why you are here, the men look at each other and shake their heads in disbelief. Even the sight of the Prince's signet ring does not change their minds. 'You would have our leader take you to Torgar?' says one, sceptically. 'You'd have him walk into a trap more likely. These tales you tell of quests and stones of power, they're 'bout as true as the uniform you wear. They all ring of deception and trickery!'

Slowly the five rise to their feet and step away from the fire, their hands drifting casually towards the hilts of their swords. On a whispered cue they unsheathe their blades and attack.

Partisans: COMBAT SKILL 24 ENDURANCE 36

You can evade combat at any time; turn to **23**. If you win the combat, turn to **170**.

217

The grisly reptile writhes and twists until, with a final tremor, it ceases its convulsions and settles into the mud. Like a hunter eager to claim a trophy, Jarel climbs astride the dead Gorodon and hacks free the two horns which protrude from its skull.

'There are potion-makers in Humbold who'll pay a grand price for these,' he says, wiping his blade on the body of the dead beast. He pockets one and offers the other horn to you.

If you wish to keep this Gorodon Horn, mark it on your *Action Chart* as a Special Item which you keep strapped to your backpack.

To continue, turn to **144**.

218

The archers are playing a game they call 'Bullseyes', but you know it better by its Sommlending name of 'Portholes'. Two diamond-shaped dice, each with ten sides numbered nought to nine are thrown by each player in turn. The numbers which appear face-up are added together (nought = zero), and the one with the greatest score wins. If anyone throws two noughts, however, they shout out 'Bullseyes!' and win automatically.

Each player must stake 12 Lune (3 Gold Crowns) per throw of the dice, and this money is bet before the dice are rolled.

Pick two numbers from the *Random Number Table* for each of the other two players and note these scores in the margin of your *Action Chart*. Now pick two numbers from the *Random Number Table* for yourself. If your total is greater than the other players you win 24 Lune. If either of the other players beats your score, you lose your stake (12 Lune or 3 Gold Crowns).

You may leave the game at any time, but you must stop playing if you gamble away all your money and cannot place your stake.

When you decide to stop playing, you return to Prince Graygor's tent; turn to **29**.

219

After several minutes of manipulation, the lock finally clicks and the door opens on to a passageway lined with torches. Half-way along the left wall you see another door – a solid slab of iron broken only by a small, barred window. Silently you approach the door and peer in through the grille.

If you have visited the Danarg in a previous Lone Wolf adventure, turn to **260**.
If not, turn to **114**.

220

As the last of the war-dogs dies at your feet, you sheathe your weapon and cast your eyes at the clearing. The bear is no longer there, having loped away during your fierce fight with the Akataz.

The pain of your wounds causes you to wince and grit your teeth as you hurry into the brightening forest. You have covered less than 100 yards when you hear a pitiful howl ripple through the trees. At first you think it is just your imagination, fuelled by fatigue and your stinging wounds. But when you hear it a second time you realize that the war-dogs you fought were part of a larger Akataz pack, and that the rest of the pack have just discovered their remains.

If you have the Magnakai Discipline of Pathsmanship and have reached the rank of Mentora, turn to **161**.
If you do not possess this skill, or have yet to reach this level of Kai training, turn to **3**.

221

A yell arises from the battlements when the defenders see Adamas appear, and a mass of boulders hurtles down to greet him. With cat-like agility he veers left and right, weaving his way through the falling rocks, which smash into the causeway with a terrific roar. He reaches the door, tears the satchel from his shoulder, and primes the crystal explosive. Automatically you begin counting the seconds as he runs back through the rubble and dead bodies. Two . . . three . . . four . . . Then your heart leaps as you see him felled by a rock and crash headlong to the ground.

If you wish to sprint forward and attempt to rescue him, turn to **138**.
If you choose to stay where you are and watch his plight, turn to **207**.

222

One of the men gets to his feet and begins walking towards you. You sense that he has not seen you, he is merely answering the call of nature, but you decide that it is wise to slip away before he gets any closer. Silently you disappear into the forest and return to the front of the building.

Turn to **89**.

223

'Identify yourself!' you shout in reply. 'Then maybe you'll hear some news that'll cheer your heart.' Slowly the man steps out from behind the boulders. He raises his hand and twenty others, maybe more, appear around the lip of the gorge. Several are armed with loaded bows, all pointed at you. The men are dressed in jerkins and breeches of crimson leather, and each carries a veritable arsenal of weapons strapped about his waist and chest. They are Eruan partisans.

'I come from the court of Prince Graygor,' you say, your voice amplified by the natural acoustics of the gorge. 'The army of Eru and the Lencian allies have driven the enemy back to Cetza. Battle is imminent and victory will soon be ours.'

'Your news is stale to our ears,' comes the reply. 'And the Prince would not send a Pathfinder to tell us such as this.' The partisans shuffle uneasily and view you with renewed suspicion. 'It is not my purpose to bring news of the war. I come to entreat the aid of Sebb Jarel,' you reply.

The spokesman for the partisans signals to the others and a section disappears from view. They reappear on horseback at the mouth of the gorge and beckon you to approach them.

If you possess a Bullwhip, turn to **185**.
If you do not possess this Special Item, turn to **342**.

224

Having made a wide detour to avoid the ford, eventually you discover an old game-trail which runs alongside the river. You follow this track for several miles until you reach a place where massive boulders, smoothed by centuries of erosion, rise out of the foaming torrent like giant stepping stones. It would be difficult, though not impossible, to cross the river at this point, but not on horseback. Reluctantly you leave your mount and make your crossing by leaping from one boulder to the next. You are half-way across when you are faced with a leap that is wider than you have ever attempted before.

Pick a number from the *Random Number Table*. If you have the Magnakai Discipline of Huntmastery and have reached the Kai rank of Primate or more, add 2 to the number you have picked.

If your total is now 6 or less, turn to **265**.
If it is 7 or more, turn to **43**.

225

The passage is flanked by burnt-out cottages, their soot-blackened walls creating a dingy corridor of an alley, which winds into the distance. Your senses tingle with the premonition of an ambush; you can almost taste the presence of the enemy lurking inside the ruined cottages. The fleeing Drakkarim halt in their tracks then turn to taunt your men, calling to them to come and fight if they dare. Before you can shout a warning, your men charge along the alley, brandishing their weapons and yelling angry cries of revenge.

If you wish to run after them, turn to **173**.
If you choose not to enter the alley, turn to **44**.

226

Jarel screams for help as he struggles to escape from the clutches of two Ciquali. They latch on to his wolfskin cloak and drag him beneath the water. He surfaces, sword in hand, but is pulled under again and this time he does not reappear. A trail of bubbles and a patch of red water drifting with the current are all there is to mark the grave of Sebb Jarel.

Turn to **97**.

227

'It's the Pathfinder,' comes the reply. 'Quick, he's wounded.'

The two soldiers run forward. They raise their shields to protect your back from the Drakkarim arrows, and help you to reach the safety of the camp perimeter, where your wounds are cleaned and dressed. Finally you return to King Sarnac's headquarters. He and the Prince are anxious to hear your report. Despite being discovered by the enemy, you have gathered useful information about the troops defending the bridge. The King praises your bravery and Prince Graygor orders his heralds to escort you back to his tent. After the ordeal of the scouting mission, you are grateful for the chance to get a good night's sleep.

Turn to **280**.

228

Forcing open your tired eyes you try to focus on the shapes as they draw closer. At first you dismiss the swirling grey figures as hallucination brought on by lack of sleep, but when a terrible chill sweeps over you like a blast of icy cold wind, fear re-awakens your senses with a jolt.

The creatures take to the air and emit a ghostly howl as they swirl around your head. You reach for a weapon but a tendril of darkness writhes out of one phantom and whips your hand. Its cold lash bites like sharpened steel and leaves your fingers numb and nerveless: lose 2 ENDURANCE points.

More tendrils appear and wriggle towards you like a host of black snakes, all of them eager to feast on your life-force.

If you possess the Sommerswerd, turn to **133**.
If you possess a Bullwhip, turn to **168**.
If you possess neither of these Special Items, turn to **74**.

229

As you dive to avoid it, the blade whistles past your shoulder, slicing open your tunic but sparing your flesh the kiss of its razor-sharp edge. Before you can rise to your feet, the Baron steps forward to deliver the *coup de grâce*. 'Victory belongs to me!' he howls, and swings his axe again. But suddenly he hears a sound that makes him recoil in horror.

Turn to **321**.

230 – *Illustration XIII (overleaf)*

You pull a metal bar set into the wall and the huge lead-lined doors rumble open to reveal an incredible sight. Before you stands a domed chamber, its ceiling criss-crossed with gantries of rusted iron. At its centre is a circular black pit around which are gathered groups of ghoulish creatures clad in transparent robes and masks. Angled upwards from the floor are slender crystal rods that glow with green fire. They pour forth a constant stream of pencil-thin light which focuses at a point directly above the centre of the pit. Your eyes are drawn to this point, for here you can see the three remaining Lorestones of Nyxator, the objects of your quest, held suspended in a ball of flickering green flame.

XIII. At the point where the crystal rods meet, the Lorestones of Nyxator hang suspended

The harsh clang of the alarm bell, and the sudden sight of you silhouetted in the doorway, has startled the creatures. They slink away from the pit and escape through an archway, leaving you and Paido alone in the chamber.

Turn to **100**.

231

'Over here!' calls Jarel, pulling open the rot-infested door of a hut at the water's edge. Inside you see an overturned rowboat with a pair of battered oars shipped underneath. He turns the small craft over and raises it by the stern.

'Give a hand,' he says, straining to push it forward. You place the oars inside, lift the bow, and help him launch it gently into the river. 'This brings back some memories,' says Jarel, wistfully. 'Though I never thought I'd ever be sharing this little booty-runner with a Pathfinder!'

You toss your pack into the boat and take your place opposite the partisan leader as he fixes the oars into position. Then, with a smooth stroke, he propels the boat out into the current and you begin your voyage towards the sinister channels of the Hellswamp.

Turn to **240**.

232

Silently you dismount and approach the charred tower door. Through the split timbers you see a man crouching beside a smouldering fire, cooking a bird that is skewered on the point of his dagger. He wears clothes cut from supple leather dyed deep crimson, and coiled on his hip you notice a Bullwhip, its braids studded with nuggets of copper.

'Join me!' he says suddenly, without raising his eyes from the glowing charcoal fire. 'There's enough meat on this fledgling for the two o' us.'

If you wish to accept the stranger's offer, turn to **129**.
If you decide to remount your horse and hurry away, turn to **75**.

233

There is a flash as your weapon smites the link and severs the amulet from the chain. The Demonlord howls and recoils, as if wounded by the blow, and you snatch the amulet away from his feet before he recovers. The black iron feels unnaturally cold; it numbs your hand and fills your arm with a dull throbbing pain. Despite your acute discomfort you know you must maintain your grip, for it is the key to the Demonlord's existence here in this temple.

Roark raises his amulet and screams a curse. Suddenly the chill that pains your arm lances across your chest and stabs at your heart. Unless you possess the Magnakai Discipline of Nexus, lose 3 ENDURANCE points.

If you survive the attack, turn to **188**.

234

Jarel appears at your side and delivers a blow that rips open the evil creature's heart. But his timely aid has diverted his attention from the forest where danger still lurks. A pair of feral eyes glint in the moonlight. Then another beast charges forward and flings itself at Jarel's unprotected back. You lift your weapon and move to strike as the creature comes flying through the air. Owing to the momentum of its attack, you have only one chance to deflect it from your companion.

Pick a number from the *Random Number Table*. If you have completed the Lore-circle of Fire, add 5 to the number you have picked.

If your total is now *0–6*, turn to **312**.
If it is 7 or more, turn to **178**.

235

The snake mistakes your movement for a hostile action and strikes out at your face.

Pick a number from the *Random Number Table*. If you have the Magnakai Discipline of Huntmastery, add 1 to the number you have picked. If you have completed the Lore-circle of Solaris, add 2 to the number you have picked.

If your total is now 5 or less, turn to **182**.
If it is 6 or more, turn to **279**.

236

You splash face-first into the mire, which fills your eyes and mouth. Blinded by the stinging mud, you fail to see your horse rear up and topple towards you, an arrow lodged deeply in his skull. His flailing hooves slam into your back and your legs are pinned beneath him when he falls heavily on his side: lose 8 ENDURANCE points.

If you are still alive, turn to **165**.

237

The ghastly creature emits a shrill whistle as you deliver your killing blow. The deadly mandibles continue to snap, but without aim or purpose, as its lifeless body slowly oozes from the hole and falls limply to the chasm floor.

Grabbing the roots firmly with both hands you haul yourself up and collapse into the undergrowth. As soon as your strength returns you gather up your equipment and advance deeper into the eerie forest.

Turn to **50**.

238

The gantry passes close enough to the Lorestones to enable you to cup your hands beneath them. If Paido were to destroy the crystal rods, the Lorestones would be freed of the energy beams and drop into your hands.

You tell Paido of your bold plan and he nods enthusiastically as you get ready to make your catch. You call to him when you are ready and, one by one, he begins to smash the crystal rods.

Turn to **196**.

239

The thunder of hooves warns you that more partisan horsemen are heading your way. You wheel your horse about and gallop down a long, twisting hill track. You are beginning to out-distance your pursuers when your steed suddenly pitches forward and throws you head-first into a tangle of foliage. The dense undergrowth cushions your fall and you emerge unscathed, but your horse has been seriously injured.

A deep pot-hole ensnared its foreleg and the limb is broken: the poor animal cannot go on. The partisan reinforcements gallop into view and you are forced to abandon your crippled mount and escape into the surrounding trees on foot. With the angry cries of the partisans echoing behind you, you curse your ill luck and hurry deeper into the darkening forest.

Turn to **250**.

240

The first day of your voyage is smooth and uneventful. The strong current bears you steadily northwards and Jarel is content to allow the boat to drift with the flow while he enjoys the warm sunshine and your conversation. You learn much about your guide and the land of Eru, and in return you recount the legends of Sommerlund and tell of your adventures in the realms of Magnamund.

At dusk you reach a confluence where the river is joined by another that flows in from the east. Here the currents are swift and treacherous, but Jarel steers the boat masterfully and brings it ashore at a muddy beach on the west bank, where a small stone hut stands close to the river's edge. You are dragging the boat up the muddy shore when Jarel suddenly freezes in his tracks. A movement among the tall grasses that fringe the beach has alerted him to a pair of green, pig-like eyes glinting in the gloom. 'Keep still,' he whispers, fearfully. 'It could be a Gorodon.' His fears are confirmed as the shadowy creature leaves its hiding place among the grasses and comes crawling down the beach towards you.

If you possess the Magnakai Discipline of Animal Control and have reached the Kai rank of Primate or more, turn to **112**.

If you do not possess this skill, or have yet to reach this level of Kai training, turn to **172**.

241

A chill of premonition runs down your spine as you stare at the old mining huts below, for you feel sure that they conceal an enemy, lying in ambush. You cast your eyes along the river for an alternative place to cross, but it is only here that the deep, fast-flowing waters of the River Brol are shallow enough to ford on horseback.

If you wish to gallop towards the ford and attempt to cross it, despite the risk of an ambush, turn to **8**.

If you choose to avoid the ford and try to cross the river further downstream, turn to **224**.

242

The first rays of dawn light are beginning to lighten the forest when you happen upon a wide gap in the trees. A dark shape, large and rounded like a furry boulder, lies curled-up beneath the branches of a pine at the edge of the clearing. In the distance a crow caws nervously, stirring the shape from its slumber with a half-hearted call of warning. Your pulse quickens as you recognize the outline of a big black bear.

A noise to your left diverts your attention from the waking bear, and to your horror you see a pack of leathery black Akataz creeping towards you through the undergrowth, their feral eyes aglow with blood-lust as they latch on to your scent. With a howl they leap forward, clawing and biting as they drag you to the ground.

If you possess the Magnakai Dsicipline of Animal Control and have reached the rank of Principalin or more, turn to **77**.

If you do not possess this skill, or have yet to attain this level of Kai training, turn to **254**.

243

You have covered twenty yards when a rain of boulders begins to crash down all around you. Suddenly a starburst of pain explodes in your head and the taste of blood fills your mouth. You fall heavily but you are numb to the pain, for your neck is broken and death is but seconds away.

Your life and your quest end here.

244 – *Illustration XIV (overleaf)*

In the company of a dozen bodyguards and court heralds, you follow the Prince as he makes his way on foot to King Sarnac's camp. It is his usual practice to inspect his soldiers on the eve of battle, to see for himself that all is well and to raise their spirits with a few words of praise and encouragement. He is heartened to discover their morale is already high and that they are all confident that he will lead them to victory.

At length you arrive at the Lencian headquarters. A huge yellow flag, bearing the emblem of a white swan and blue dragon, flutters in the breeze above the royal tent where a unit of silver-clad knights stands stiffly

XIV. On a detailed map of the town, the Prince and the King mark the places where their regiments will assemble and attack the enemy

to attention. A trumpet announces your arrival and the knights escort you inside to meet the King. After formal greetings have been exchanged, the grey-haired King begins to discuss the impending battle. The Prince has brought with him a detailed map of the town and, as the two leaders formulate their plans, it is used to mark the places where their regiments will assemble and attack the enemy.

'If only we knew the number of reinforcements Baron Shinzar has received,' says the King, uneasily. 'Then we could be sure our plans would succeed.' The Prince nods in agreement. 'We must send a scout to reconnoitre their defences, or hundreds of our soldiers could lose their lives needlessly in the assault.'

The King looks in your direction then returns his eyes to the Prince. 'I have no scouts trained for such a delicate operation,' he says, 'but I see you have a Pathfinder. Send him. His skills would be well suited to this task.'

The Prince hesitates. He cannot reasonably refuse the King's suggestion, yet to send you into the enemy camp would endanger your life and your quest.

If you wish to volunteer to scout the enemy positions, turn to **53**.
If you choose to remain silent, turn to **171**.

245

A dozen webbed hands slap over the gunwales and six ghoulish, dome-shaped heads rise dripping from the river. A rasping croak issues through their bared fangs when they see you are prepared for their attack, and frantically they try to clamber into the boat before you can cut them down.

Ciquali: COMBAT SKILL 21 ENDURANCE 36

Increase your COMBAT SKILL by 2 points for the duration of the fight due to your readiness to receive the attack.

If you win and the fight lasts four rounds or less, turn to **169**.
If the fight lasts longer than four rounds, turn to **309**.

246

You succeed in slowing the effects of the venom now coursing through your veins. But you have been bitten by a Yua and its bite is fatal unless treated immediately with the only known antidote – Oede herb.

If you possess some Oede herb, swallow it to neutralize the venom and turn to **205**.
If you do not possess any of this rare herb, turn to **343**.

247

Casting your eye across the body-strewn terrain, you soon realize that all the riderless horses are now either dead or have fled the field in panic. Left with no alternative, you scramble out of the mud and set off after the Prince on foot.

Turn to **115**.

248

As soon as your light illuminates the darkness, the phantoms emit a venomous hiss and swirl away into the shadows. They are afraid of the light but their need to feed on your life-force will soon overcome this fear unless you can devise a more permanent way of keeping them at bay.

If you possess the Magnakai Discipline of Psi-surge, turn to **281**.

If you do not possess this skill, turn to **55**.

249

The corroded iron gantry creaks violently as you inch your way nearer to the ball of green flame, and, eventually, you reach a position where the Lorestones are within your grasp. But as you stare at the flickering core of energy you realize that to touch it would be fatal.

You ponder the problem for several minutes before you hit upon a solution.

Turn to **238**.

250

You run without pausing through the shadowy pines until you can no longer hear the cries of your pursuers. The forest is soon swallowed by the night but, guided by your Kai senses and the occasional rays of moonlight that filter through the densely packed trees, you are able to continue your lonely trek eastwards. You stop at a stream to bathe your face in the cold water and reflect on the bitter irony of your situation: the people you had hoped would help you now pursue you as their enemy. It is a cheerless situation but you do not allow it to defeat your resolve to reach Torgar and recover the stolen Lorestones.

Gradually, what begins as a suspicion becomes a nagging certainty that you are being watched. Your senses detect an evil presence lurking in the surrounding trees and you decide to forego rest and keep moving until dawn. Tired and hungry after your ordeal, you must now eat a Meal or lose 3 ENDURANCE points.

Turn to **242**.

251

The swarthy-faced warriors loose their arrows as they advance, but they are poorly aimed and whistle past to splash harmlessly in the river. The leading attackers seem impressed by your display of courage and they slow down. You take advantage of their hesitation and launch yourself at them, catching them wrong-footed as you land your first blows.

Zagganozod: COMBAT SKILL 24 ENDURANCE 35

Owing to the impetus of your attack, add 2 points to your COMBAT SKILL for the first round of combat.

If you win the fight, turn to **271**.

252 – *Illustration XV*

You unsheathe the sun-sword and flames course along the blade, filling the ruins with its vivid golden light. The Prince turns to shout a warning but his adversary strikes him a cruel blow that lays open his thigh and hurls him to the ground. Although his helm hides his face, its nose-bar and chin-piece exposing little but a malicious glint in his eyes, you are sure that this is no ordinary Drakkarim warrior; the smell of evil hangs heavy around him like the stench of a rotting corpse.

He snarls a vile curse and flings his sword at your head.

XV. The Drakkarim warrior thrusts the stave of iron at your chest and a blast of white flame scorches your arm

You fend off the spinning blade with ease but the attack has served its purpose. The warrior snatches up the shimmering iron rod and it hums with a force that reveals its ancestry: it is a stave of power forged in the furnaces of Helgedad. With a mighty yell he thrusts the stave at your chest and a blast of white flame scorches your arm as you parry the attack on the hilt of the Sommerswerd. Half-blinded by the flash, you stagger back and quickly muster your strength for a desperate fight to the death.

Ziran (with Powerstave):
COMBAT SKILL 40 ENDURANCE 50

The Ziran is immune to Mindblast (but not Psi-surge).

If you win the combat, turn to **305**.

253

The flames burn ferociously and you lose 5 ENDURANCE points before you are able to extinguish them.

If you survive your burns, turn to **318**.

254

Their attack is so swift and deadly that there is no time to draw a weapon. The gruesome clack of their fangs fills your ears and white-hot pain lances through your arms and legs as the Akataz snap shut their powerful jaws: lose 6 ENDURANCE points. Desperately you kick and punch, rolling over and over through the undergrowth until you break free of their crushing bite. Weak from loss of blood, you stagger to your feet and unsheathe a weapon just in time to meet their renewed attack.

Akataz: COMBAT SKILL 27 ENDURANCE 43

These war-dogs are especially susceptible to psychic attack. If you have and wish to use the Discipline of Mindblast or Psi-surge, double all bonuses you would normally receive. If you have completed the Lore-circle of Spirit, triple all bonuses.

If you win the combat, turn to **220**.

255

You are able to identify many of the flowers that fill the gorge. Among them are the blue and pink blooms of the Lacaress, used throughout Magnamund as an active ingredient of sleeping potions. It is the insidious scent of these flowers that is slowly numbing your senses. Wary of the danger, you rein your horse about and hurry out of the gorge.

Turn to **98**.

256

You draw your weapon and strike out at the phantoms, but your blows pass through them harmlessly. They howl with fiendish glee as they swirl around your head, whipping you with tendrils of darkness that writhe like thin black snakes from their filmy bodies. Every lash weakens your Psi-screen and you sense that if you are to survive this merciless assault you must quickly find a weapon to combat these fell creatures of the night.

If you possess a Bullwhip, turn to **168**.
If you possess a Kalte Firesphere, a Torch and Tinderbox, or a Lantern, turn to **248**.
If you possess none of these items, turn to **24**.

257

You lie for several minutes, semi-unconscious due to the stunning impact: lose 6 ENDURANCE points. Gradually your senses return and you stagger to your feet. Every muscle in your body aches viciously, but no bones are broken, and you are filled with relief that you have not ended your days like those whose mouldering remains carpet the chasm floor.

You examine the hollows that riddle the walls and conclude that they were made by a burrowing animal of some sort. Most are too small to enter, but there is one that is large enough to explore.

If you wish to enter this bore-hole, turn to **141**.
If you wish to attempt to climb the chasm wall, turn to **135**.

258

Using your Kai skill you intensify your vision. The distant ruins grow larger and clearer and you can see a figure crouched upon the highest point of the broken temple wall: it is a warrior clad in silver mail and a gold-spiked helmet. He raises a plain rod of iron and another crackling bolt of blue-white fire leaps from its tip to strike the pikemen with lethal accuracy. Their screams of terror rend the air and the survivors fall apart in a desperate, panic-stricken flight to escape the fate that has befallen their slain comrades. Quickly you inform the Prince of what you have seen at the temple.

Turn to **42**.

259

It feels good to have firm ground beneath your feet once again, even though it is no more than a crusty mud flat supporting a brace of stunted trees. Jarel ties the boat to one of the twisted trunks and settles down to sleep while you take the first watch. Your rumbling stomach reminds you that you have not eaten today: you must eat a Meal now or lose 3 ENDURANCE points.

The night sounds of the swamp make you uneasy but your watch passes without event. Shortly after mid-night, Jarel awakens and you are able to catch a few hours' sleep before dawn arrives and you take to the water once more.

Turn to **101**.

260

Beyond the door you see a dank dungeon cell. A prisoner sits crosslegged on the cold stone floor, his head resting on his chest. The dark skin on his hands and arms is covered in tiny scars, and his plaited hair is matted with grime and dried blood. Wearily he raises his head and your pulse races as you recognize the face of Lord Paido, warrior-magician of Dessi.

Turn to **278**.

261

As the Death Knight screams his last oath and falls face-first into the stinking ditch-water, you hear shouting and the sound of men in armour descending the bank from both sides of the bridge. Drawn by the sounds of your struggle, the elite Drakkarim warriors are closing in for the kill. Speed is your only ally now. With an energy born of desperation, you claw your way up the slippery bank and sprint towards the allies' encampment. The enemy see you escaping and direct a hail of arrows at your fleeing figure. Two shafts bury themselves in your back (lose 12 ENDURANCE points) and you are pitched to the ground.

If you are still alive, turn to **203**.

262

Waves of psychic power wash over your mind and leave you shaking with shock. Your Psi-screen protects your nervous system but you are unable to stop the waves from penetrating deep into your memory. Lord Adamas increases the power of the mind-gem until you reveal your true identity and the nature of your quest.

Turn to **290**.

263

'Hear me, O Lord of Pain,' cries the leader. 'Your humble servant Roark invokes you to aid him in this hour of dread uncertainty. Come forth and conquer. Come forth and feast upon the souls of our enemies!'

As the grim words uttered by the grey-haired figure echo through the temple, your Kai senses detect a stream of invisible force rising from the marble block. Gradually the force takes the form of a mist filled with ghastly apparitions. An icy chill engulfs the temple as the mist swirls like a cyclone around the walls.

'Come! Come, Tagazin!' screams Roark, his voice barely audible above the howling wind. 'From the pit of eternal pain I summon thee!'

If you possess the Magnakai Discipline of Divination and have reached the rank of Mentora, turn to **298**.

If you do not possess this skill, or have yet to reach this level of training, turn to **116**.

264

A terrible pain rips through your body: you gasp in shocked surprise and instinctively clutch your body. Blood oozes thickly between your fingers and you stare down in horror at the arrow which is protruding from your chest. Colours whirl and sounds grow faint as the pain drags you to the ground. Then, as the agony reaches an intolerable pitch, the pain suddenly disappears and you plunge into the timeless oblivion of death.

Your life and your quest end here.

265

The wind whistles past your face as you leap across

the gap and land with a jolt that leaves you breathless. Desperately you cling to the rock, but your feet cannot grip the smooth surface and you slip backwards into the river.

You surface quickly but the river here is deep and strong, and you cannot resist being swept along on the current. For over three miles you ride the icy white water until you begin to feel smooth rocks speeding past beneath your feet. By kicking out against these boulders you are able to propel yourself towards the bank. Cold and exhausted, you claw your way out of the water and collapse on the rocky shore.

Your fall and the rough river ride have taken a toll of your possessions. Delete the items you have listed fourth, fifth and sixth on the Backpack section of your *Action Chart*, and half the contents of your Belt Pouch.

To continue, turn to **294**.

266

A figure dressed in black robes, whom you recognize as one of Roark's followers, is waving a burning torch in front of him at arm's length and shouting. Five spectral shadow-shapes wreathed in mist swirl around him, trying repeatedly to penetrate his fiery guard. Behind him stands an ancient burial mound, and lying near its dark entrance are the bodies of two soldiers clad in leather armour and three horses. A dozen of the ghost-like apparitions hover over each of the soldiers, as if they are feasting on their bodies.

If you possess the Magnakai Discipline of Divination and have reached the rank of Mentora, turn to **303**.

If you wish to help the black-robed man fight off his ghostly attackers, turn to **71**.

If you choose to avoid this conflict, skirt around the edge of the quarry and continue deeper into the forest, turn to **175**.

267

'That ring you're wearing and those clothes o' yours look real enough,' he says, flicking the bird meat from his dagger, 'but you don't look like a Pathfinder and you sure don't sound like one neither!' Then, without warning, he draws back his blade and flings it at your throat.

Pick a number from the *Random Number Table*. If you have the Magnakai Discipline of Huntmastery, add 3 to the number you have picked.

If your total is now *0–4*, turn to **208**.
If it is *5* or more, turn to **33**.

268

As you hurry away you happen upon a trail that gradually descends to the bank of a rushing river. Massive boulders, smoothed by the water over the centuries, rise from the foaming torrent like giant stepping stones. Across the river you see another forest, dark and forbidding. The sun is strong in a cloudless sky and the air is warm and dry, yet a grey mist hangs heavy and cold around the trees of that forest.

All along the bank on this side of the river grow clumps of bushy herbs with bright scarlet flowers.

If you have the Magnakai Discipline of Curing, turn to **276**.

(continued over)

If you do not possess this skill, turn to **325**.

269

The Vakeros is overjoyed at the prospect of being rescued from this dreadful place. He has languished here for a year since being captured by agents of the Darklords. His name is Paido, and although you tell him that you are an Eruan Pathfinder, he recognizes your accent and your strong Sommlending features.

'You may wear Eruan cloth but you are not a native of that land,' he says, suspecting that you have been sent to trick him.

If you wish to reveal your true identity to this man, turn to **69**.
If you do not, turn to **337**.

270

The enemy are rallying to launch a counter-attack on the hill. To the south you see a mass of leather-clad Hammerlanders, supported by a regiment of grim-faced Brigandi mercenaries, advancing towards the Prince's position. The Palace Guard have fought like lions, but they have lost half their number and must be near to exhaustion. They may not survive a counter-attack by a much fresher force that outnumbers them five to one. All that can save them now are the Eruan reserves.

If you wish to take command of the Prince's reserves and march them towards the hill, turn to **49**.
If you decide to ride to King Sarnac's camp and ask him to save the Prince, turn to **197**.

271

Wiping the sweat from your brow, you sheathe your weapon and search the bodies of your ambushers. All of them are clad in black helmets and scarlet, chain-mail hauberks, and each has an assortment of weapons and equipment strapped to their muscular bodies. You recognize the distinctive armour which identifies them as Zagganozod – a motley unit of Drakkarim cavalry which patrols the Blackshroud Trail. This company must have fled here on foot after the Drakkarim defeat at Cetza, for you can find no sign of their horses.

Your search of their bodies reveals the following items:

2 SWORDS
3 QUIVERS
2 DAGGERS
11 ARROWS
3 BOWS
2 AXES
1 MACE
1 BROADSWORD
16 LUNE (4 Gold Crowns)
ENOUGH FOOD FOR 4 MEALS

You may take whatever items you wish. When you have made the necessary adjustments to your *Action Chart*, you ford the river and continue on foot.

Turn to **186**.

272

Your arrow strikes the Baron, but he is saved from a fatal wound by the lip of the steel bevor that protects his neck and back. The arrow ricochets, gouging a deep furrow across the base of his skull and making him fall heavily to his knees. Bellowing like an angry bull, he glares in your direction as he staggers painfully to his feet.

If you possess the Sommerswerd, turn to **113**.
If you do not possess this Special Item, turn to **126**.

273

You take your place beside Lord Adamas and charge through the smouldering gap, leaping over the charred and broken remains of the Drakkarim who were caught by the blast. The allied soldiers follow your lead and sweep into the startled city, through a gate now guarded only by the slain. Despite their shock, the defenders begin to rally as they receive fresh reinforcements from other parts of the city, and soon a vicious battle rages in the cramped, gloomy streets.

You lead a group of Palmyrion men-at-arms across a courtyard and into a dingy street where you find yourselves confronted by a regiment of Drakkarim garrison troops. They have gathered to make a wall of shields behind a pair of small figures, black-robed and cowled, each holding a yellow globe.

If you possess the Magnakai Discipline of Divination and have reached the rank of Tutelary or more, turn to **22**.

If you do not possess this skill or have yet to reach this level of Kai training, turn to **57**.

274

Desperately the two men fight to defend themselves from your deadly attack. You cannot evade this combat and must fight them both to the death.

Pirsian Swordsman 1:
COMBAT SKILL 18 ENDURANCE 31
Pirsian Swordsman 2:
COMBAT SKILL 17 ENDURANCE 29

If you win the combat, turn to **68**.

275

'My mission is secret,' you reply. 'If it is to succeed it is vital that it remains so.' You glance at the other men seated around the fire and they return your glance with suspicion.

'They are my brothers. Whatever you wish to say to me can be said in front of them.'

If you wish to tell these men about your quest, turn to **216**.

If you would prefer not to tell them anything, turn to **51**.

276

You recognize the plants: they are Laumwort, a herb very similar to the healing plant, Laumspur. You can regain lost ENDURANCE points by eating the leaves.

Each Meal of Laumwort restores 2 ENDURANCE points and there are enough leaves here for 3 Meals. If you decide to pick this herb and keep it, remember to adjust your *Action Chart* accordingly.

To continue, turn to **325**.

277

The sniper's second arrow splinters harmlessly against the wall behind which you shelter. Close to where you lie is the crimson-splashed body of a Drakkarim Death Knight. Wounded during the fighting at the bridge, he crawled here to die. A Broadsword and an Axe hang from his belt, and among the contents which have spilled out of his pack you see a Bottle of Water, a Torch, a blanket and enough food for three Meals.

You may take any of these backpack items or weapons before leaving the ruins and pressing on towards the centre of the town.

Turn to **155**.

278

A key to the cell door hangs on a hook nearby. You grab it, twist it in the lock, and kick the heavy slab of metal. It creaks open and Paido rushes forward to embrace you.

'Thank the Gods you have found me, Lone Wolf,' he says, his voice filled with emotion. 'The Drakkarim said you were dead, that your body lay rotting in the Danarg, but I never once believed their lies.'

Paido is overjoyed to hear that the Torgar Gate has fallen and that a battle is raging in the streets above.

And when you inform him of your mission he replies with news that raises your hopes of success.

Turn to **307**.

279

Your lightning reflexes save you from the snake's deadly bite. Its jaws snap shut around air and instantly it recoils into its hollow in case you retaliate. Rather than attempt to kill the snake in the tight confines of the shaft, you snatch the opportunity to escape.

Turn to **205**.

280 – *Illustration XVI (overleaf)*

At the break of dawn the soldiers of Lencia and Eru rouse themselves and adopt their positions for the fight. You gather your equipment and join the Prince at the top of the hill on which he has established his command post. He is observing the enemy line through a telescope and dictating orders to his heralds, who commit his words to parchment and dispatch them to his regiments in the field.

'We outnumber the enemy two to one, but they are well positioned to receive our attack,' comments the Prince, handing you his telescope so that you can scan their lines.

The town of Cetza is little more than a handful of ruined cottages clustered on a flat-topped hill. To the north lies a wood and a small hill on which a ruined temple stands; to the south lies an orchard surrounded by a low wall, and further on, open grassland bisected by a ditch that runs the whole length of the battlefield. The road from Luomi crosses the ditch at a stone bridge

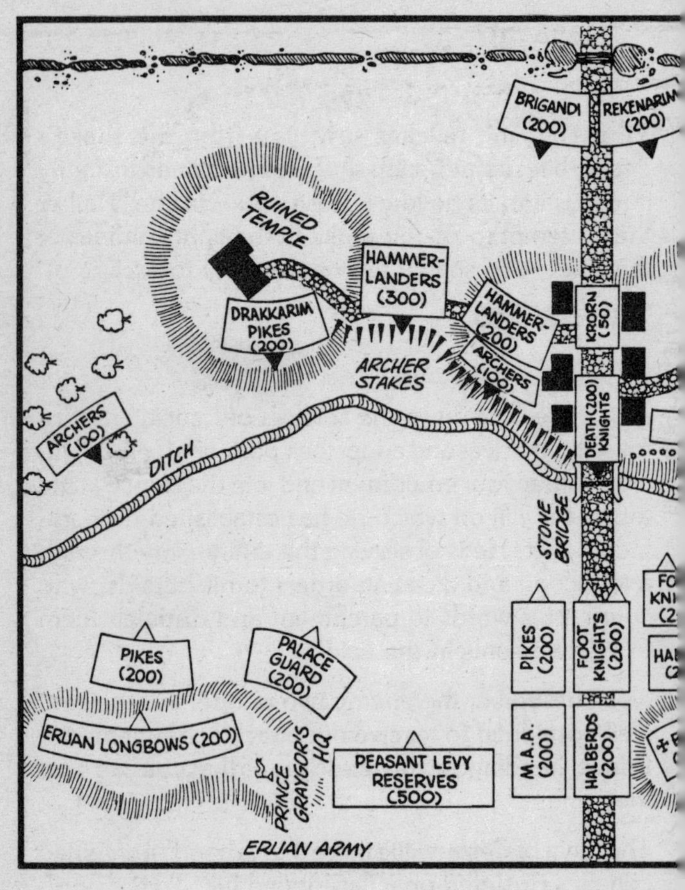

XVI. The Battle of Cetza: Troop positions at dawn

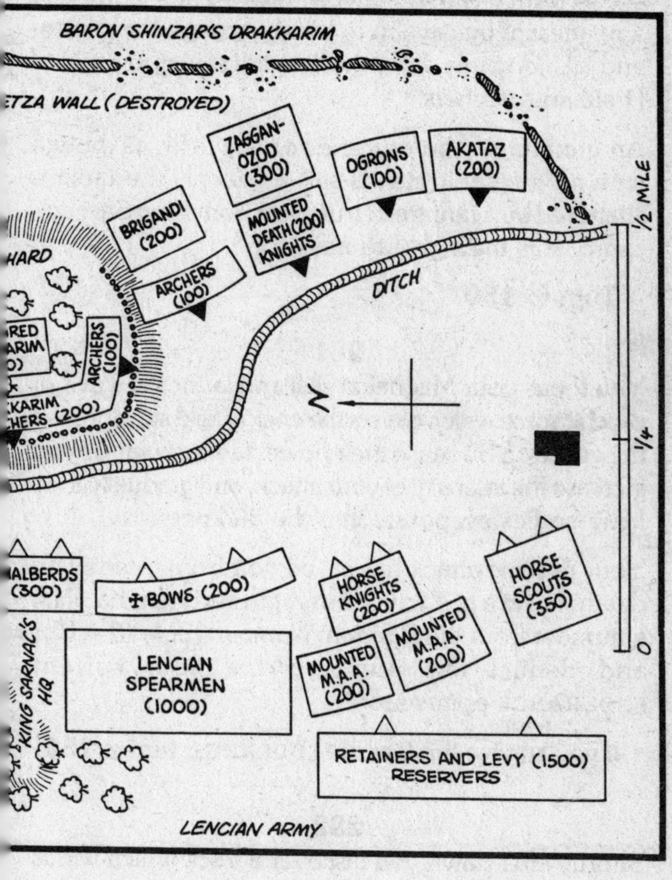

BARON SHINZAR'S DRAKKARIM
ETZA WALL (DESTROYED)
ZAGGAN-OZOD (300)
OGRONS (100)
AKATAZ (200)
BRIGANDI (200)
MOUNTED DEATH (200) KNIGHTS
ARCHERS (100)
DITCH
ARCHERS (100)
N
1/2 MILE
1/4
0
ALBERDS (300)
✠ BOWS (200)
HORSE KNIGHTS (200)
HORSE SCOUTS (350)
MOUNTED M.A.A. (200)
MOUNTED M.A.A. (200)
LENCIAN SPEARMEN (1000)
KING SARNAC'S HQ
RETAINERS AND LEVY (1500) RESERVERS
LENCIAN ARMY

which is barricaded and heavily defended. The enemy have also been busy to the north. A mass of pointed stakes form a barrier between the two hills to impede any attempt by cavalry to break through the centre, and all along this defensive line are row upon row of Drakkarim archers.

An unnatural calm descends on the field, as though time momentarily stands still. Suddenly the quiet is shattered by a fanfare of trumpets from King Sarnac's camp. It is the signal to advance.

Turn to **150**.

281

You focus your Magnakai skill and launch a wave of psychic force which batters the energy field surrounding the ghosts. You sense their power fading away as you increase the intensity of your attack, and gradually their filmy bodies evaporate into the darkness.

Your psychic attack has saved you from a terrifying death, but at a cost to your strength and stamina. Pick a number from the *Random Number Table* (*0* = *10*), and deduct this number from your current ENDURANCE points score.

If you survive this loss of ENDURANCE, turn to **156**.

282

Shortly after dawn you discover a track which winds its way northwards through the rough-barked pines. 'This old game-trail will lead us down to Smuggler's Nook,' says Jarel, chewing on a piece of dried meat he has pulled from his pack. 'I reckon we should get there this side o' noon.'

His prediction comes true, for it is mid-morning when you arrive at a ragged group of plank huts on the bank of a fast-flowing river. At one time these shanties were the thriving centre of illegal trafficking in gold and gems. The citizens of Pirsi, who mine these rich resources in the Eru Range, used to smuggle their precious cargoes out of the country by boat, choosing to risk the dangers of the Hellswamp rather than pay the Prince his taxes. It was only after the Prince decreed the death penalty for such smuggling, and employed Pathfinders to help enforce his law, that the Pirsians finally gave up their illegal trade.

Turn to **231**.

283

A black-shafted arrow gouges a furrow of skin from your forearm and knocks you backwards out of the saddle: lose 3 ENDURANCE points. Your horse panics and gallops away, disappearing over the brow of the ridge as you stagger to your feet. Then, with a harsh yell, your ambushers pour out of the log hut. They are eager to finish you before you can offer any resistance. Three of them are armed with bows which they reload as they advance towards you.

If you wish to evade them by wading across the ford, turn to **166**.

If you have a bow and wish to use it, turn to **131**.

If you wish to draw a hand weapon and prepare for combat, turn to **251**.

284

As the Palace Guard advance majestically, their serried ranks of steel slowly change formation in preparation for the Prince's order to charge. Heavy lances rise like the spines of a steel porcupine and their scarlet and yellow pennons unfurl to the wind. A wave of arrows comes flying towards you, sent by the Drakkarim standing behind their fence of stakes, but the range is long and the black shafts rattle harmlessly off Eruan armour and shields.

The first rank of horsemen reach the ditch to find the earth soft and waterlogged. The ruined temple lies 300 yards ahead, and before it a line of Drakkarim pikemen stand grimly silent on the slope of the hill. A war horn blares its signal and suddenly all hell breaks loose. Arrows pour down on all sides: from the enemy archers to the right and from archers, previously unseen, lurking in the woods to the left. Many shafts find their way through the sides of helmets and between plates of polished armour. Still the Prince commands his men onwards and they force their horses across the ditch, braving the savage hail of death. You survive the arrows and steer your horse through the cloying mud, but you are knocked from the saddle by a riderless steed maddened by the pain of its wounds.

Pick a number from the *Random Number Table*. If you have the Magnakai Discipline of Animal Control and Huntmastery, add 3 to the number you have picked.

If your total is now *0–4*, turn to **236**.
If it is *5* or more, turn to **183**.

285

Beyond the staircase lies a circular parapet which

overlooks a huge, cavernous crater. It is filled with thousands of human slaves toiling with pick and shovel deep in the sulphurous heart of Torgar. Their bodies are filthy and covered with sweat despite a freezing wind, which howls in the depths like a hungry wolf. Drakkarim overseers urge them to greater effort, and the crack of their whips is answered by the slaves' anguished cries of pain.

Angered by what you have seen, you leave the parapet and enter a dimly lit passage that descends to a door of black steel. A twist of the handle reveals that it is locked.

If you have a Black Key, turn to **80**.
If you have a Skeleton Key, turn to **219**.
If you possess neither of these Special Items, turn to **130**.

286

You draw your golden sword, and its cleansing light washes over the Demonlord's unwholesome form. He growls uneasily, as if sickened by the close proximity of such a noble blade, and slowly he withdraws into the temple. Roark and his followers huddle in the corner and watch with fearful eyes as their master prepares to attack.

Demonlord Tagazin:
COMBAT SKILL 45 ENDURANCE 65

This supernatural being is immune to Mindblast (but not Psi-surge).

If you reduce his ENDURANCE to 20 points or less, do not continue combat but turn instead to **20**.

287

'Very well,' says the captain. He looks towards the bar and shakes his head. Your muscles tense as you get ready to dive to the floor but, to your relief, all you hear is the owner placing his crossbow on the counter. 'I shall take you to Jarel, but you must agree to wear a blindfold: it's a safeguard, for your own good as well as his. If you were to be captured and tortured by the enemy, you would be unable to tell them where the partisans are encamped.'

He summons the owner, who produces a square of black cloth from his pocket and winds it around your eyes. The captain leads you outside and helps you on to your horse and the two of you set off along a secret forest trail. After two hours in the saddle you reach your destination and the blindfold is removed.

Turn to **25**.

288

You fight with breathtaking skill and every blow you land leaves an enemy dead at your feet. 'Pull back!' you shout, as you cut and thrust at the snarling Hammerlanders. 'Pull back to the bridge!'

Gradually the survivors extricate themselves from the ambush and run back along the alley, leaving just you and two Lencian knights to cover the withdrawal. A knot of Hammerlanders, armed with axes, scream their blood-curdling war-cry and rush forward to hack you down.

Hammerlanders:
COMBAT SKILL 29 ENDURANCE 40

Add 2 points to your COMBAT SKILL for the duration of the fight, for you are helped by the Lencians fighting by your side.

If you win the combat, turn to **44**.

289

The collision with the far wall leaves you breathless but otherwise unharmed. Gripping firmly with both hands, you haul yourself out of the chasm, untie the stick from the end of your rope and wind it back into your pack before setting off deeper into the eerie forest.

Turn to **50**.

290

'So you are the one they call Lone Wolf,' he says, thoughtfully. 'And you have come here to break into Torgar and claim that which belongs to you. How strange it is that our goals should be so similar. Come, follow me, perhaps co-operation will hasten our success.'

Turn to **127**.

291

It is soon after sunset when you arrive at Pirsi. Fog swirls through the gloomy streets and crooked alleys, but you can see light seeping from chinks in the reinforced shutters and doors of only a few of the cabins. You bring your horse to a halt and dismount beside the steps of a large log hut that serves as both a general store and tavern. Your steed neighs uneasily, drawing your attention to a group of stony-faced men who are advancing along the street. Torches blaze in their work-worn hands, casting a vivid yellow glow in their suspicious eyes as they approach you warily. Their leader, who is dressed in the uniform of an Eruan Pathfinder captain, steps to within inches of your face. Coldly he stares into your eyes, his jaw set in a rigid sneer of contempt.

'Have you forgotten how to salute, soldier?' he growls, menacingly. 'Or perhaps you're not a Pathfinder after all. Perhaps you're just another skulking Drakkar spy?' You notice that several of the men carry Bor pistols, primitive but very deadly weapons, especially at such close range. If you are to save your skin you had best salute the captain immediately.

If you choose to salute by touching your forehead, turn to **193**.

If you choose to salute by raising your hand, palm outwards, turn to **60**.

If you choose to salute by placing your hand across your chest, turn to **7**.

292

The fight raging on the hill becomes a vicious struggle as the Hammerlanders hurl themselves like hungry wolves at the battle-weary Guard. Doggedly you advance until you are close enough to shout the charge. Then, with a rousing cheer from the Prince's men to speed them on their way, your command rush forward and the leading pikemen take the enemy in the flank. The attack is devastating. The Hammerlanders and the Brigandi are split in two and swept from the hill like autumn leaves. The pikemen halt and you order the archers forward to fire into the retreating enemy.

The retreat becomes an all-out rout as the enemy flee the battlefield in chaos.

Turn to **66**.

293

The two diminutive magicians see you level your bow and realize that they are in danger. As you take aim, they get ready to hurl their spheres at the Palmyrions.

Pick a number from the *Random Number Table*. If you possess the Magnakai Discipline of Weaponmastery, add any bonuses you have to this number.

If your total is now *7* or less, turn to **149**.
If it is *8* or more, turn to **164**.

294

The sun is strong in the cloudless sky and it quickly dries your sodden clothes and warms your aching limbs as you stand surveying your new surroundings. A stony trail leads into a forest of mist-enshrouded trees and, despite the heat of the sun, you feel a sudden chill of premonition. Instinctively you know that this is the Isle of Ghosts Prince Graygor spoke of so fearfully.

With caution guiding your every step you follow the trail, treading carefully through saw-briar that tears mercilessly at your boots and breeches, until you are forced to stop at the edge of a narrow chasm that bisects the trail. A tangle of yellowed bones lies at the bottom and a damp, unwholesome smell rises from a number of tiny caves that riddle the sheer walls.

If you wish to attempt to jump across the narrow chasm, turn to **123**.
If you wish to look for a way around it, turn to **62**.

295

The cold blue light of early morning and the sound of a crow cawing in the distance stir you from your deep sleep. Rays of golden sunlight stream through the forest's canopy, illuminating the dark, grey-green foliage and making your continued trek through the pines a far easier task than last night. You make excellent progress and at mid-afternoon you emerge from the woods that fringe the eastern border to find yourself staring at the River Brol and the rolling green sea of trees that is the Moggador Forest.

The rushing waters of the Brol are too deep to traverse at this point, so you follow the rock-strewn bank northwards until you catch sight of an ideal place to cross. The remains of an ancient bridge, which collapsed centuries ago, form a shoal of broken stones that ford the river. The water bubbles and foams as it washes over this shallow causeway. Eagerly you approach the ford, but you stop dead in your tracks when you hear gruff, inhuman voices coming from a clump of bushes near the river's edge.

If you have the Magnakai Discipline of Invisibility or Pathsmanship, turn to **194**.

If you do not possess either of these skills, turn to **67**.

296

Roughly you pull the dead Drakkar on to his stomach and cut open his pack. In his pack and on his body, you discover the following items:

SWORD
DAGGER
BOW

BLANKET
QUIVER
3 ARROWS
16 LUNE (4 Gold Crowns)

You may take any of these items before pressing on towards the centre of the town.

Turn to **155**.

297

The Palace Guard succeed in closing their ranks and fending off the frenzied attacks of the desperate Drakkarim. Their gallantry and battle-skill is a stirring sight as they fight their way determinedly towards the crest of the hill. Faced by such noble warriors, the Drakkarim begin to falter and fall back in disarray towards the town.

As you near the top of the hill you catch sight of Prince Graygor. He is locked in mortal combat with a silver-clad warrior inside the ruins of the temple. Strewn around them are the dead bodies of the Palace Guardsmen who, with the Prince, broke through the Drakkarim pikemen during their charge upon the hill. The Prince is trying to prevent the warrior from retrieving a rod of iron that lies on the ground between them. This rod crackles with a blue-white fire that shimmers along its length.

If you possess the Sommerswerd, turn to **252**.
If you do not possess this Special Item, turn to **143**.

298

A tingling sensation electrifies your senses and fills your mind with images of events which took place in this temple thousands of years ago. So strong are the psychic residues that linger here that the images appear breathtakingly vivid.

During the Age of the Old Kingdoms, when the Elder Magi ruled the land, this temple was a place of learning and experimentation. It was here they developed their knowledge and understanding of nature, and many beneficial discoveries were made to the betterment of Magnamund. The guardians of this laboratory were a Drodarin race called the Patar. They served the Elder Magi and in return they were entrusted with their new-found secrets of herbcraft and druidic lore. But the Patar betrayed that trust when they allowed the Cenerese, a clan of evil druids, into the temple to plunder its secrets. The Cenerese called upon their Demonlord, who appeared in this very chamber. He took all that the Elder Magi had nurtured and cultivated, and he turned it against them in the form of a deadly plague that decimated their race. In the wake of their destruction, the Cenerese and Patar rose to power, but their reign was short-lived. A clan of goodly druids called the Herbalish, who had helped the surviving Elder Magi to escape their enemies during the years of the Great Plague, waged war on the Cenerese and were victorious.

The Patar fled the temple in shame and gave a solemn pledge to the Herbalish that they would redeem their act of treachery by devoting themselves to the study of the healing arts and by striving to defeat disease in all its forms. Ever since, the descendants of the Patar have been known as the Redeemers, and each new generation has upheld that ancient vow.

But the story has yet to find an ending, for in this forgotten temple you are now witnessing a terrifying repeat of history. Roark and his followers are Cenerese druids and they have come here once more to invoke the help of their master – the Demonlord Tagazin.

Turn to **116**.

299

The alarm bell signifies that the entrance to the tower is under attack. Adamas and his army have reached the centre of the city and are now fighting their way down into the dungeons in an attempt to free the slaves. The Death Knights are hurrying to their battle stations and they are unaware of your presence in this chamber.

Turn to **136**.

300

A triumphant cheer fills the air as the soldiers of Prince Graygor and King Sarnac flood into the square; Cetza has been recaptured and the enemy have been smashed beyond recovery. Everywhere you look there are joyous faces, for the death of Baron Shinzar has sealed a victory that will liberate all of Eru from the cruel yoke of Drakkarim occupation.

As you watch the defeated remnants of the enemy escape across the ruins of the Cetza Wall and scurry like rats for the safety of Blackshroud, Prince Graygor joins you in celebration of the victory. 'We have triumphed, Lone Wolf,' he says. 'Our land is now free and the way is open for you to reach Torgar and fulfil your quest.'

Turn to **4**.

301 – *Illustration XVII*

The crystal explodes with a blinding flash, releasing a bolt of sun-like energy that tears a massive hole in the one-foot-thick iron plate and transforms what little remains into red-hot slag. The shuddering concussion jars the entire causeway and fragments of glowing metal fall all around you. Triumphant cheers rise above the thunderous boom that is rumbling through the ravine, as the spearpoint of Adamas's army surges across the causeway towards the ruined gate.

Turn to **273**.

302

The sergeant's request is not as innocent as it seems, for he recognizes the copper nuggets that are woven into the braids of the Bullwhip. He knows of only one such whip and its owner would not have parted with it willingly. You sense that several of the other partisans also recognize the whip and are slowly edging their horses nearer in order to surround and attack you.

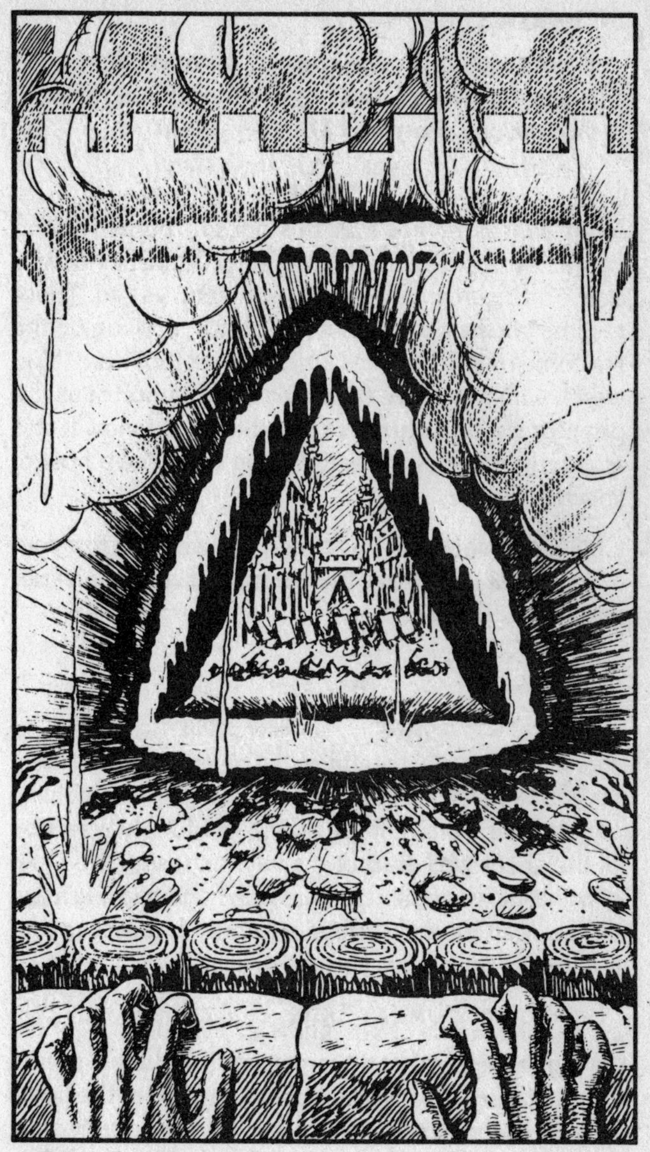

XVII. A massive hole is torn in the iron plate and the spearpoint of Adamas's army surges towards the ruined gate

If you wish to evade combat, turn to **39**.

If you choose to stand your ground and fight the partisans, turn to **118**.

303

Your senses reveal that this ancient burial mound contains the evil spirits of 100 Cener druids, who were slain and incarcerated here many centuries ago. These restless ghosts haunt the wooded isle, preying on the life-force of any humans who dare set foot here. You watch with a mixture of fascination and horror as the phantoms gradually overcome the robed follower and attach themselves to his twitching body like a host of spectral leeches.

Chilled by what you have seen and anxious to avoid a similar fate, you leave the quarry and venture deeper into the dark forest.

Turn to **175**.

304 – *Illustration XVIII*

The jolt leaves you breathless but otherwise unharmed. As you recover your composure you hear a scrabbling sound deep within the rockface. Suddenly a section of the sheer wall crumbles away, exposing the head of a ghastly worm-like creature with huge clacking mandibles. You have disturbed a hungry Lapillibore and it is intent on eating you alive.

Lapillibore: COMBAT SKILL 16 ENDURANCE 50

Owing to your precarious position, deduct 3 points from your COMBAT SKILL for the duration of the fight. To prevent yourself from falling into the gorge you can fight using only a weapon that can be used with

XVIII. The head of a ghastly worm-like creature with huge clanking mandibles is exposed

one hand (a sword, mace, axe, dagger, short sword or warhammer).

If you win the combat, turn to **72**.

305

At the moment of his death, a cone of black fire erupts from the stave and engulfs the Ziran's body. The guttering ebony flames howl like a pack of demons as they form into a small cyclone and ascend into the sky. Swiftly you take hold of the injured Prince, heave him across your shoulder and carry him away from the black tornado that is sucking chunks of temple debris into its spinning core.

Once you are a safe distance from the temple, you lower the Prince gently to the ground and watch the cyclone ebb and fade.

Turn to **211**.

306

A dozen horses, bridled and furnished with coverings of black and gold, stand tethered to an obelisk of stone. Two leather-clad soldiers sit nearby, sharing a pipe of aromatic tobacco as they gamble at cards. They each wear an emblem on their shoulder, which is also embroidered upon the horse's saddle cloths: it is a gold portcullis on a black crest.

If you have travelled the Stornlands of Central Magnamund in a previous Lone Wolf adventure, turn to **65**.

If you have never been to the Stornlands, turn to **222**.

307

'I can help you, Lone Wolf,' he says, his warrior pride restored by the thought of avenging his cruel imprisonment. 'I know where the Lorestones are being held and I will take you there.'

Turn to **88**.

308

Since the first rays of dawn light brightened the eastern sky, the streets of Luomi echoed to the shouts of sergeants and the crunch of booted feet. The regiments of Lencia and Eru are taking their places in the column of march, and by mid-morning this column, 6500 strong, is ready to leave for battle. Company by company, through the city's east gate, they depart, tramping the dusty road that leads to Cetza. When the time comes for you to join them you take your place with Prince Graygor's escort and fall in line behind the armoured knights of the Palace Guard.

The army is well protected by Lencian horse scouts before, behind and on both sides, to make sure it is not ambushed whilst crossing the twenty miles of open grasslands to Cetza. During the afternoon a troop of scouts are sent ahead to spy on the enemy. They return to report that Baron Shinzar has fortified the town and received reinforcements from Blackshroud since his defeat at Luomi. The news does not cheer Prince Graygor, for he knows the ground around Cetza does not favour the attacker.

It is dusk when the army arrives on the outskirts of the town. In the gloom you can see the enemy campfires flickering between the ruins of cottages that were destroyed when the Drakkarim first invaded this land. Occasionally their gruff voices can be heard on the chill evening wind as they shout orders and call the names of slaves and attendants. After a whole tiring day's marching, and with night drawing close, the order goes round that there will be no battle offensive this evening. Quickly the regiments disperse and many fires are lit. Tents are erected for the knights and the baggage carts are unloaded to provide the men with stores that should make their night in the open less uncomfortable. The Prince chooses to position his headquarters on a hill to the north that overlooks the town, and King Sarnac of Lencia chooses a similar position on a hill beyond the road, half a mile to the south. Shortly after the tents are constructed, a message arrives from King Sarnac's headquarters, inviting the Prince to join him and draw up plans for tomorrow's battle. The Prince accepts the invitation and says that you may accompany him if you wish.

If you wish to accompany the Prince to King Sarnac's headquarters, turn to **244**.
If you choose to decline the invitation, turn to **90**.

309

As you dispatch the last of the amphibians, Jarel grabs hold of the oars and begins to row with all his might. But you have covered only a short distance when there is a loud crack and a sharpened wooden stake rips through the bottom of the boat. The tiny craft rocks violently as a tall fountain of water gushes through the torn planks. Then suddenly the boat capsizes and you are pitched head-first into the murky river.

A webbed hand claws your leg (lose 2 ENDURANCE points) but you kick out savagely and break free of its clammy grip. Free of your unseen attacker, you strike out for the south bank and drag yourself, cold and shaken, up on to the muddy shore.

Turn to **226**.

310

The axe bites into your side as you dive to avoid it. You roll with the blow, tumbling over when you hit the ground to lessen the shock of impact, but the wound you have suffered is severe and you are too weak to rise immediately: lose 8 ENDURANCE points.

If you are still alive, turn to **321**.

311

You draw a weapon and slap the sole of Jarel's boot to awaken him.

'What the. . . !?' he splutters, as he sits up and rubs his sleepy eyes. But before you can say anything, you hear another of the fish-like things; it is behind you, clambering over the upturned boat. You spring to your feet and Jarel just manages to unsheathe his sword as the creatures attack simultaneously.

Bhakish: COMBAT SKILL 21 ENDURANCE 28

These swamp dwellers are immune to Mindblast (but not Psi-surge).

If you win the combat, turn to **34**.

312

You lash out and the beast twists in mid-air as your

blow hits its side. But the wound you have dealt it is superficial and not enough to deter it from attacking. It lands close to Jarel and immediately regains its balance to leap again. This time its intended victim is not your companion: it is you.

Taintor Wolf (wounded):
COMBAT SKILL 21 ENDURANCE 36

If you win the combat, turn to **178**.

313

Stoically your horse climbs the difficult track out of the valley towards the crest. You hope to catch sight of your destination from this ridge of high ground, but because of the lush foliage you can see little of what lies ahead. Densely packed trees and bushes reduce visibility to less than a dozen yards.

It strikes you as the perfect environment for guerrilla warfare, and you can readily understand how Sebb Jarel and his partisans have managed to ambush and evade the Drakkarim so effectively for two years. Further along the narrow trail you come across the grisly remains of one such ambush. A score of severed

Drakkarim heads, still encased in skull-like helms of black iron, have been impaled upon a line of wooden stakes. They serve as a grim warning of what awaits any Drakkar who dares to venture beyond this point.

You are hungry and must now eat a Meal or lose 3 ENDURANCE points before you continue further.

Turn to **291**.

314

A strong aura of evil and treachery pervades the entire area, and your senses detect that you are not alone – the building is occupied. Forewarned by your psychic skills, you avoid approaching the clearing. Under cover of the dense undergrowth you make your way around to the rear of the building where you witness a curious scene.

Turn to **306**.

315

Few of the creatures have any hair and their gnarled brown skin is as shiny as oiled leather. They shuffle forward awkwardly on short bowed legs, their mouths hanging open to reveal rotten fangs and swollen purple tongues. Their leader fixes you with a cruel stare as he orders his warriors to attack.

Krorn: COMBAT SKILL 23 ENDURANCE 35

If you win the combat, turn to **84**.

316

Swiftly you scramble out of the ditch and sprint back along the road towards the allies' encampment.

'Zaj gaz! Zaj gaz!' howl the Drakkarim defenders as they catch sight of your shadow-like form, and a clutch of black arrows hiss through the air. One clips your shoulder and another gouges your leg (lose 4 ENDURANCE points) but you fight the pain and run on without making a sound that could direct an arrow to your heart.

Fifty yards from the allies' picket line you see two Lencian men-at-arms moving towards you with their swords drawn. 'Give the password!' they shout. 'Give the password or perish!'

If you answer, 'Shortsword', turn to **63**.
If you answer, 'Longsword', turn to **347**.
If you answer, 'Broadsword', turn to **227**.

317

Before attempting the jump, you cut away the briars that might otherwise ensnare your feet and pitch you head-first into the gorge. The gap is a little over twelve feet wide, but with a clear run-up you feel confident you can traverse it in one bound. The only disadvantage is the weight of your equipment.

If you wish to remove your backpack and weapons and throw them across the gorge before you jump, turn to **27**.
If you choose to jump whilst carrying your equipment, turn to **103**.

318

Less than half of the Palmyrion men-at-arms have survived the devastating attack. They reel back towards the courtyard and you manage to pull them into a circle just in time to defend against the Drakkarim who are charging along the street.

Drakkarim Garrison:
COMBAT SKILL 26 ENDURANCE 39

If you win the combat, turn to **332**.

319

Your Kai senses save you from the sniper's shaft: it whistles past harmlessly as you dive for cover. As you rise to your feet you spot your would-be assassin hastily reloading his bow.

If you have a bow and wish to use it, turn to **36**.
If you choose to evade the sniper by running along an alley to your left, turn to **155**.

320

The advancing Death Knights skid to a halt when they see you emerge from the shadows. 'Ruzzar!' bellows their leader, and quickly they unsheathe their swords and attack.

Elite Death Knights:
COMBAT SKILL 42 ENDURANCE 48

If you win this combat, turn to **162**.

321

A trumpet announces the arrival of Prince Graygor's men as they swarm around the west side of the square. Baron Shinzar screams in anger and lifts his axe on high, daring them all to step forward and feel its lethal caress. His offer is met by a dozen arrows, loosed by Eruan archers from the houses bordering the square, but the shafts are drawn to the blade of the sorcerous axe where they disintegrate in a sizzling splash of glowing splinters. With an evil laugh, the Baron mounts his charger and gallops through the soldiers, cutting down those brave enough to stand in his way. But as he leaves the town he finds his escape blocked by a new and formidable enemy.

Turn to **110**.

322

Swiftly you dive beneath the bridge and wait with bated breath as the horsemen approach. They thunder across the bridge, and when you can no longer hear their hoofbeats pounding the rocky road, you climb out of your hiding place and continue northwards.

Turn to **179**.

323

Again a crackling bolt of blue-white fire lances from the hill-top ruins and strikes with lethal accuracy. Screams of terror rend the air as the [illegible]ain soldiers fall apart in a desperate, panic-stricken flight to escape the fate that has befallen their slain comrades. Your Kai senses draw your eyes away from this carnage to focus on a figure clad in silver mail and a gold-spiked helmet. He is crouching on the highest point of the dilapidated temple wall and you sense that his magical power is the source of the deadly blasts. Quickly you inform the Prince of what you have sensed and seen at the temple.

Turn to **42**.

324

Using your powers of telescopic vision you focus on the ruined log huts and scan them for signs of life. A dull glint of sunlight on tarnished steel and a glimpse of a scarlet-clad figure moving behind an open doorway warn you that the settlement is occupied. You cast your eyes along the river for an alternative place to cross. But it is only here that the deep, fast-flowing waters of the River Brol are shallow enough to cross on horseback.

If you wish to gallop towards the ford, despite the risk of an ambush, turn to **8**.

If you choose to avoid the ford and try to cross the river further downstream instead, turn to **224**.

325

Carefully you cross the raging river, leaping from one boulder to the next. The sun warms your body but you feel an unexpected chill as soon as you set foot on the opposite bank. Instinctively you know that this is the Isle of Ghosts Prince Graygor spoke of so fearfully.

A stony trail leads into the heart of the mist-enshrouded trees. It is partially overgrown with saw-briar, which tears mercilessly at your boots and leggings. Undaunted, you press on until forced to stop at the edge of a narrow chasm that bisects the trail. A tangle of yellowed bones lie at the bottom and a damp unwholesome smell rises from a number of tiny caves which riddle its sheer walls.

If you wish to attempt to jump across this narrow chasm, turn to **123**.

If you wish to look for a way round it, turn to **62**.

326

You snatch the amulet from Roark's lifeless hand and then turn to confront Tagazin. You sense an energy flowing between Roark's amulet and the amulet that hangs around the Demonlord's neck, and you use this power-bridge to ward off the creature.

Tagazin shudders as your psychic commands rob him of his supernatural strength. His body becomes pale, almost transparent, and wisps of smoke curl from his skin as though his body was evaporating slowly. He retreats towards the centre of the temple and leaps on to the marble block. There is a chilling howl and suddenly the shadowy chamber is flooded with a blinding light. Thunder booms and the walls shake. Terrified, Roark's followers flee the temple and scramble up the stairs. Crackling bolts of white lightning leap from the marble block to tear great chunks of rock from the walls, and the air seethes with a cloying stench that threatens to suffocate you. With terror in your heart you bound up the steps and escape as the defeated spirit of the Demonlord vents its spite on the chamber below.

Turn to **341**.

327

You return to consciousness with a throbbing headache. A circle of bristle-bearded faces swim in and out of focus, staring down at you as if you were a fish in a bowl. You try to rise but are discouraged from doing so by the point of a sword that hovers above your heart. As your vision slowly clears you realize that you are no longer in the gorge, and the faces you see belong to a company of crimson-clad partisans.

'It was careless of you to wander into Lacaress Gorge, Pathfinder,' says a tall, lantern-jawed sergeant. 'What were you hoping to find there save a good night's sleep?'

'I came with Prince Graygor's leave,' you say, showing your signet ring as proof. 'I am here on a secret mission of great urgency. I must speak with your leader, Sebb Jarel.'

The sergeant inspects your ring carefully. 'Very well,' he says, and sheathes his sword. 'We shall take you to Sebb, but you must agree to be blindfolded.' You nod your assent and a yard of cloth is wound about your eyes. Guided by the sergeant, you are helped on to your horse and the reins given into the hands of one of his men. After two hours in the saddle, you reach your destination and the blindfold is removed.

Turn to **25**.

328

You focus your Kai skill on the detent, willing it to move aside. It clicks back and the door opens on to a passage lined with torches. Half-way along there is another door – a solid slab of iron broken only by a small, barred window. Silently you approach this door and peer in through the grille.

If you have visited the Danarg in a previous Lone Wolf adventure, turn to **260**.
If you have not, turn to **114**.

329

Blinking the sleep from your eyes, you scramble to your feet and reach to your weapons. 'Stand back to back,' whispers Jarel, his keen eyes peeled for a sign of the beast among the densely packed trees. You remember hearing tales of the Taintor wolves during your travels through Eru, of their cruelty, speed and savage cunning. At the time you thought the stories were greatly exaggerated, but now you are not so sure.

'There, over there!' hisses Jarel, pointing to a knot of pines with the tip of his sword. A scream rises from the darkness, which becomes a howl, high-pitched and horrible. The dark foliage rustles, then a massive wolf-like creature bursts into view and runs towards you, its eyes rolling and its long, yellow fangs gaping wide.

If you have a bow and wish to use it, turn to **70**.
If not, turn to **187**.

330

When he opens his fist you see that the coin shows 'heads'. 'Fate has chosen you for this heroic task, Kai lord,' he says, and hands you the leather satchel containing the crystal explosive. 'My men will cover you with their crossbows when you make your run. Place the device so that the shard faces the door and remember, you have only ten seconds to get back once it is activated.'

You shoulder the satchel and, as Adamas gives the order to his men to fire, you scramble over the rampart and sprint towards the great iron door.

Pick a number from the *Random Number Table*. If you have the Magnakai Discipline of Huntmastery, add 2 to the number you have picked. If you have completed the Lore-circle of Solaris, add a further 2.

If your total is now *0–1*, turn to **243**.
If it is *2–7*, turn to **99**.
If it is *8* or more, turn to **184**.

331

'I see you wear the Prince's mark,' he says, pointing at your signet ring with the tip of his blade. 'Be you running an errand on his behalf?'

'Aye,' you answer, mimicking the Eruan accent to perfection with the help of your Kai Discipline. 'An errand of great urgency. Do you know where I might find Sebb Jarel?'

The man laughs and slaps his thigh. 'Aye, that I do,' he says, jovially. 'He's my brother. You'll find him encamped at the foot o' Hawkridge Mountain. Stay on the trail to Pirsi until you reach the old mining settlement of Kaig. Then take the track that follows the stream. Just keep on ridin' and you'll find ol' Sebb soon enough.'

You thank him for his help and hospitality and turn to leave. As you reach the doorway he calls out: 'Be watchful when you enter the forest. There's a pack o' Akataz on the loose. If they catch scent o' your horse they'll be down on you quicker than lightning.'

Turn to **75**.

332

The surviving Drakkarim scatter into the surrounding alleys and you are able to advance towards the centre of Torgar unopposed. The Palmyrions meet up with their regiment and you continue alone along the dingy thoroughfare. It leads to an open square where a conical tower of iron points accusingly at the sky. Here the flagstones vibrate to a continuous throbbing that beats like a gigantic pulse somewhere deep in the bowels of the city. The battle has drawn most of the Drakkarim away from this square and you have no difficulty in reaching the tower and entering it via an open archway. A corridor of steel lies beyond, empty save for the constant din that assails your ears. Countless passages lead off from the main corridor, all sloping downwards, and many occupied by Drakkarim warriors. The passages are poorly lit and it is easy to avoid your enemies until you reach a vast stairway bathed in a bright orange glow that radiates from a level below.

Pick a number from the *Random Number Table*. If you have completed the Lore-circle of Solaris, add 3 to the number you have picked.

If your total is now *0–6*, turn to **348**.
If it is 7 or more, turn to **47**.

333

With one swipe of his huge white paw, he hooks his claws into your tunic and flings you across the temple. Shocked by his speed and ferocity, you scramble to your feet and fumble for a hand weapon as he stalks after you like a cat teasing a frightened mouse. His face is set in a ghastly sneer as he enjoys the novelty of his mortal form.

Around his neck, on a chain of black iron, hangs an amulet forged in the shape of a fiery, five-pointed star. You notice that Roark possesses a similar amulet which he clutches to his chest as if his very life depended on it. He and his followers are huddled in a corner of the temple, watching you and their master fearfully.

If you wish to attack the Demonlord with your weapon, turn to **210**.
If you wish to try to cut the amulet from his neck, turn to **128**.
If you wish to attack Roark and take the amulet he is holding, turn to **41**.

334

Seconds after leaving the ditch, another hail of deadly arrows whistles down and you are forced to dive for cover to avoid being hit. When you rise once more it is to the sight of your horse rearing up on his hind legs and scrabbling the air frantically with his fore-hooves. An arrow has pierced his skull and you watch with sorrow as he topples and crashes lifelessly into the mud.

All the other riderless horses are either dead or have fled the field in panic. Left with no choice, you scramble out of the mud and set off after the Prince on foot.

Turn to **115**.

335

Swiftly you cross the rocky causeway, taking care to tread on only those stones that rise above the foaming white torrent, and you enter the Moggador Forest as quickly as the dense trees will allow. The ground rises steeply and it is dusk before your climb ends at the crest of a ridge overlooking the Isle of Ghosts. In less than an hour it will be dark, so you decide to camp here on the ridge and continue at first light (you must now eat a Meal or lose 3 ENDURANCE points).

You are preparing to settle down on a bed of leaf mould when the howl of a timber wolf prompts you to abandon your soft mattress and spend the night in the bough of a tree.

Turn to **125**.

336

Your arrow creases the creature's skull and disappears into the darkness beyond. It howls at the sudden pain but does not cease its attack. The wolf is now upon you and there is no time to draw a hand weapon to ward off the first snap of its great yellow fangs.

Taintor Wolf: COMBAT SKILL 26 ENDURANCE 46

You must fight the first round of combat unarmed. At the start of the second round you may draw a weapon (if you possess one) and fight the beast as normal.

If you win and the fight lasts four rounds or less, turn to **202**.
If the fight lasts longer than four rounds, do not continue but turn instead to **234**.

337

'What manner of deceit is this?' he growls accusingly. 'Know you this, your tricks and your tortures will never break my spirit, for I am of the Vakeros and we are slave to no man!'

Your Kai senses tell you that he is speaking the truth – he is a Vakeros warrior-magician of Dessi. Certain now of his truthfulness, you decide to reveal to him your real identity.

Turn to **69**.

338

The Death Knight warrior appears, his huge black form silhouetted in the archway. You grip your weapon tightly and prepare to strike him a fatal blow should he see you hiding in the shadows, but you do not need to attack. He snatches up the spear in his mailed fist, turns and hauls himself out of the ditch, grunting and cursing his carelessness as he struggles in his heavy armour.

You wait twenty minutes before leaving the bridge and working your way slowly along the ditch.

Turn to **124**.

339

The officer looks at you as if you are insane. 'The crazy fool thinks he's a Kai lord,' he says scornfully to his men as he climbs back into his saddle. 'The foul air of this wilderness has addled his brains. Let us ride on; we've wasted too much time here already.'

He spurs his horse forward and you are forced to dive aside as the riders surge across the bridge and disappear along the road that leads to the Moggador Forest.

Turn to **179**.

340

With your heart pounding fit to burst, you gulp a lungful of air and leap into the gorge. For a few seconds you lose your orientation as you tumble in the air then you hit the river with a stunning crash: lose 4 ENDURANCE points.

You soon surface but the current is very strong and you cannot resist being swept along. For over a mile you ride the icy white water until your feet touch some smooth rocks as they speed past below. By kicking out against these boulders you are able to propel yourself towards the bank. Cold and exhausted, you eventually claw your way out of the water and collapse on the rocky shore.

The jump and your river ride have taken their toll of your possessions. Delete the items you have listed second, third, fifth and seventh in the Backpack section of your *Action Chart*. Also, delete half the contents of your Belt Pouch and one Special Item of your choice.

Turn to **294**.

341

Dust clogs your throat and the roar of falling stone is deafening as you race towards the surface. When you reach the ramp that leads to the crystal doors you find it split wide open. A web of cracks zig-zag across the two halves and a growing mound of rubble threatens to seal off the exit. Desperately you claw your way across this jagged debris, passing the bodies of some of Roark's followers, and diving through the shrinking exit just before the ceiling collapses with a tremendous crash.

Outside the situation is remarkably calm; only a slight ground tremor and a sound like distant thunder hint at the incredible destruction taking place inside the temple. The clearing is deserted and you are beginning to think you are the only one to have escaped, when you hear horses galloping away and glimpse three riders disappearing along a track that heads off to the east. It is nearly dark and they are soon swallowed by the shadows of the forest.

If you wish to follow them, turn to **181**.
If you choose to ignore them and spend the night in the clearing, turn to **19**.

342

As you approach the partisans you hold up your right hand to display your signet ring. It is enough to convince them that you speak the truth.

'Very well,' says their sergeant, a tall lantern-jawed man with iron-grey hair. 'We shall take you to our leader. But you must agree to wear a blindfold. It is for your own good as well as ours. The Drakkarim torture their prisoners: should you fall into their hands you'll not be able to tell them where we are encamped.' He pulls a length of cloth from his saddlebag and wraps it tightly around your eyes. Then another takes hold of your reins and leads you away from the gorge. After two hours in the saddle you finally reach your destination and the blindfold is removed.

Turn to **25**.

343

A creeping numbness paralyses your limbs and, as your fingers lose their strength, you cannot prevent yourself from falling into the bore-hole after the Black Yua that injected you with its deadly venom.

You survive the fall but the strength of the venom ensures that you will never escape from the shaft.

Your life and your quest end here.

344 – *Illustration XIX (overleaf)*

With devastating speed and accuracy, you draw your arrows and fire them deep into the hearts of the two enemy archers. Both men stagger and crumple to the ground, but your bowmanship does little to deter their comrades. With a fearsome yell, the three remaining warriors brandish their swords and axes and come thundering towards you. There is no time to evade their attack – you must fight them to the death!

Zaggonozod: COMBAT SKILL 20 ENDURANCE 32

If you win the combat, turn to **271**.

345

On the other side of the alley is a line of burnt-out cottages. Their soot-blackened walls are mostly intact, although their roofs have long been open to the sky. The fleeing Drakkarim are beginning to out-distance your men and you fear they will get away, when suddenly they halt and turn to face you.

At that instant a mass of leather-clad Hammerlanders emerge from the cottages, rending the air with their howling battle-cries. They strike your men from every side, catching them like helpless fish in a barrel.

If you wish to stand and fight your attackers, turn to **288**.

If you wish to try to escape from this ambush, turn to **16**.

346

A group of high-ranking warriors are gathered around a table on which lies a map of Ghatan and the Hammerlands. They are engrossed in their plans for an assault

XIX. The three remaining warriors brandish their swords and axes and come thundering towards you across the causeway and they do not notice you enter the tent. The officer speaks with one of the lords, who leaves the table to come and question you.

'Welcome Pathfinder,' he says, his keen eyes glinting like two polished gemstones. 'I am Adamas, Lord Constable of Garthen, commander-in-chief of the Talestrian army. What news do you bring from Eru?'

Rather than risk raising his suspicions, you tell him of the Eruan-Lencian alliance and their successful struggle against the forces of Baron Shinzar of Blackshroud. He listens with interest to your report, then he asks how you came to be 200 miles from Prince Graygor's army.

If you have the Magnakai Discipline of Divination, turn to **86**.

If you do not possess this skill, you can either say that you are on a secret mission; turn to **158**.

Or reveal your true identity; turn to **290**.

347

The shouts of the Drakkarim and the rain of their arrows unnerves the guards. They fear it is the prelude to a night attack, and when they see a black-clad figure stumbling towards them and hear him give the wrong password, they panic. 'Enemy attack!' they shout, waking a unit of crossbowmen stationed on the high ground behind. They rush to grab their loaded weapons and take aim at the enemy, but the only target they can see is you. 'Fire at will!' commands their sergeant.

A scything wave of iron bolts lifts you off your feet and a terrifying pain tears through your chest. You are mortally wounded and, although you fight to hold on to life, it is a struggle you cannot win.

Your life and your quest end here.

348 – *Illustration XX*

When you are half-way down the staircase a shadow looms into view. Seconds later a Drakkar officer appears and begins to ascend. He is the most repugnant human being you have ever seen. His enormous bloated body bulges with over-developed muscles to the point of deformity and his face is puffy and fat, shiny with sweat, and pitted with disease. A battle wound on his right cheek has scarred badly, drawing that side of his face into an ugly sneer. He sees you and unsheathes a massive, saw-edged scimitar as he strides up the stairs and attacks.

Drakkar Assault-Captain:
COMBAT SKILL 31 ENDURANCE 35

If you win the combat, turn to **177**.

349

Your arrow passes clean through the creature's mouth, tearing a jagged hole in its furry jowl. The beast shrieks at the sudden pain and shakes its head, spraying you with thick crimson blood. Maddened by the pain, it snaps its great fangs and rolls its grim yellow eyes as it steadies itself to pounce on you and exact its revenge.

Hurriedly you drop your bow and unsheathe a hand weapon as the wolf springs towards your chest.

Taintor Wolf: COMBAT SKILL 25 ENDURANCE 42

XX. A Drakkarim officer appears – the most repugnant human being you have ever seen

If you win and the fight lasts four rounds or less, turn to **202**.

If the fight lasts longer than four rounds, do not continue the combat but turn instead to **234**.

350

'Vengeance is mine, Lone Wolf!' booms the thunderous voice. Terror strikes deep in your heart when you turn and see the ghastly form of Darklord Gnaag, filling the archway through which his minions escaped when first you entered this chamber. A ghastly rasping laugh echoes from his fly-like head as he raises a black crystal and points it at the gantry. 'The vow I gave at Tahou shall be fulfilled. Now I shall destroy you and the Lorestones!'

There is a deafening crack and a bolt of blue lightning streaks from the stone held in his pincer-like claw. It shears through the rusty metal and you are peppered with red-hot iron splinters. As the shock wave hits the weakened ball of fire, the two Lorestones are sent

tumbling into the black abyss. Then a second bolt from the black stone tears the gantry in two, and with the ghastly laugh of Darklord Gnaag ringing in your ears, you plummet headlong into the icy cold pit.

You have fallen into a portal of total darkness, a shadow gate that leads to the twilight world of Daziarn. The wisdom and strength of the Lorestone of Luomi is now a part of your body and spirit, and the last remaining Lorestones are still within your reach, but your descent into the Daziarn heralds the beginning of a deadly, supernatural episode of the Magnakai Quest.

If you have the courage of a true Kai master, the wonders and the horrors of the twilight plane await you in book 11, the penultimate Magnakai adventure, entitled:

THE PRISONERS OF TIME

RANDOM NUMBER TABLE

4	0	4	8	7	4	0	9	7	5
7	6	3	6	9	6	5	6	0	2
5	8	9	3	8	0	4	7	4	5
2	7	0	4	6	8	2	5	6	4
4	8	2	4	2	3	8	2	9	5
8	2	6	8	6	7	9	8	2	8
3	0	8	4	6	1	3	5	6	9
8	0	2	7	3	5	1	7	9	4
3	8	6	5	8	1	6	8	2	6
0	8	4	6	1	0	1	6	9	5